The Coming
of the Bear

The Coming
of the Bear

A NOVEL

Lensey Namioka

HarperCollins*Publishers*

Typography by Joyce Hopkins
1 2 3 4 5 6 7 8 9 10
First Edition

Library of Congress Cataloging-in-Publication Data
Namioka, Lensey.
    The coming of the bear / by Lensey Namioka.
       p.   cm.
    Summary: Two unemployed samurai are saved from drowning by the Ainus, a primitive people on a northern Japanese island, and are torn in their loyalties when the possibility of war arises between the Ainus and a band of Japanese settlers.
    ISBN 0-06-020288-2. — ISBN 0-06-020289-0 (lib. bdg.)
    1. Ainu—Juvenile Fiction. [1. Samurai—Fiction. 2. Japan—Fiction. 3. Ainu—Fiction.] I. Title.
PZ7.N1426Co 1992   91-17331
[Fic]—dc20   CIP
                                                                            AC

To the Namiokas of Hokkaido

LIST OF CHARACTERS

ZENTA, a ronin, or unemployed samurai
MATSUZO, his friend

The Kotan
The headman of the Ainu group
The hunter, elder brother of the headman
TONKURU, younger son of the headman, his
designated successor
ASHIRI, elder son of the headman
MOPI, daughter of the headman
The wife of the headman
OKERA, wife of Ashiri

The Settlement
COMMANDER KATO
The steward
SETONA, foster sister of the commander, half Ainu
JIMBEI, one of the settlers

The bear

The Coming
of the Bear

"Do you think that's China over there?" asked Matsuzo. The young samurai asked the question idly. They had been two days without food, one day without water, and he was light-headed. He didn't even suffer from the cold anymore.

Their boat had been adrift for more than a week. Yesterday they had had a moment of excitement when they caught sight of land again, but since that time, they hadn't seemed to be getting any closer to the shore. The coastline was still only a dark smudge in the distance.

"It's unlikely to be China," replied Zenta. "We've been going more or less in a northerly direction.

I'm not quite sure what that coast is—it could be some country we know nothing about." His voice held only a hint of hoarseness, and his eyes were still clear. Having spent more years of hard living than Matsuzo, he was better able to endure starvation and cold.

Matsuzo found that he didn't particularly care whether the coastline they saw was China or some exotic country inhabited by naked savages. Weakened by cold and hunger, he knew the shore was too far away to reach by swimming, anyway. He looked up languidly at a sea gull flying overhead. "Maybe I can persuade that bird to land on the prow. Then I'll catch it and wring its neck. A nice plump bird can feed us both." In fact he wasn't sure he had the energy to wring the bird's neck, even if he could talk it into sitting still for him.

Zenta began to rummage through their belongings. They had left Mutsu so hurriedly that they had taken next to nothing with them. Having made a powerful enemy, the two men had been advised by their friends to leave without delay. In the middle of the night, they had rushed down to the harbor, where a small boat had been made ready for them. There was enough food and drink in the boat to last them a week. As to weapons, they had their own swords, as well as two bows and quivers filled with arrows.

This would have got them safely to a neighboring province, with provisions to spare, if it had not been for a sudden, disastrous squall. The storm had blown them far out into the Sea of Japan, but what was worse, they had lost their oar.

Zenta struggled to string his bow. Matsuzo noted that privation had sapped some of his strength as well.

"What are you going to do?" asked Matsuzo, sitting up.

Zenta looked over his arrows. "You wanted a nice plump bird, didn't you?"

"You're not going to try to shoot one?" asked Matsuzo. "Even if you hit it, the bird will fall into the sea!" He felt a return of energy. Unfortunately, it made his thirst much worse.

Zenta selected his arrow and notched it. "Not if I time it right." He let the arrow fly just as the boat tilted, and missed.

Zenta shot another arrow, and missed again. However skillful he was, it didn't seem possible that he could hit a flying bird from a moving boat.

"You'll use up all our arrows," said Matsuzo. "What will you do if we meet some unfriendly Chinese?"

Zenta took out another arrow. "We need food to give us energy, but we need liquid even more.

A sea gull could give us both. Besides, if we should be unfortunate enough to land in China, a few arrows more or less won't make much difference."

The gulls seemed to be laughing at Zenta's attempts. They flew closer and mewed sarcastically. Then one of them suddenly plummeted straight down.

"Got him!" Zenta reached out and frantically tried to hook the fallen bird with the end of his bow. But the bird had fallen into the water and out of reach. Doggedly, he notched another arrow, and this time he carefully studied the speed and direction of the flying birds.

Totally engrossed in the swooping sea gulls, the men did not notice that a sudden wind was rising, driving their boat sharply toward the shore. Nor did they notice several human figures standing by the beach, staring intently at them with farsighted eyes.

Matsuzo lay back again, but a thud at his feet made him open his eyes. A bleeding bird lay with an arrow through its chest.

"Well?" demanded Zenta. "Aren't you going to wring its neck?"

Zenta's eyes were bright with a glitter that made him look not quite sane. It must be thirst, thought Matsuzo. His own throat seemed to be filled with burning twigs. He swallowed with difficulty, and reached gingerly for the bird.

Before Matsuzo could pick up the dead sea gull, a lurch of the boat threw him against the gunwale. Wincing, he turned and saw that Zenta had also been sent sprawling, and was painfully picking himself up. Again the boat lurched.

Rubbing his head, Zenta looked up. "Hold on! We're in for another storm."

The sky had turned black, and the boat began tossing so violently that the two men knelt down and clung grimly to the sides with both hands. "We're headed straight for the shore!" cried Zenta.

Matsuzo could barely hear his words in the howling wind. He nodded, for by now he too had seen the coast bearing down on them.

Neither man saw the figures running along the shore, shouting and pointing at their tossing boat.

Huge, glistening rocks suddenly loomed in front of them. There was a shriek of wood grating against rock, and a bone-shaking crash tore their hands from their hold. Matsuzo's world turned upside down. The icy waves lashed at him like whips. He felt a burning pain on his right calf. Something struck his head, and a roar filled his ears. He saw streaks of white and gold.

Some time later—he didn't know how much later—he found himself retching while someone held his head. It was cold, so cold. The ground was hard and rocky—he was on firm ground at last, although it had a tendency to tilt treacherously. Then a cup was held to his lips. It contained fresh, sweet water, but at first his lips were trembling so much that he could not keep them at the rim of the cup. At last he was able to swallow, and found the water to be the most delicious he had ever tasted. He drained the cup and sighed. Then, cold as he was, he lay down and went to sleep.

When Matsuzo opened his eyes again, he saw blue sky and gulls flying overhead. For an instant he thought he was back on the boat, and that the storm and the crash against the rocks had been a nightmare. Then he became aware of a scratchy feeling against his neck. A cover had been drawn over him, a blanket made of some coarse material.

"You're awake," said Zenta's voice. "How do you feel?"

Matsuzo struggled to sit up. As he raised his head, a hot streak of pain flashed across his forehead, and he closed his eyes again. "Bumped my head against something," he muttered.

"You certainly have," agreed Zenta. "Unless a prodigious hen has laid an egg on your head. Would you like some more water? I won't offer food just yet."

Water? Food? So they had arrived safely on land! And they must have encountered friendly, hospitable people. Ignoring the pain now thumping through his head, Matsuzo opened his eyes wide and looked around. He was lying on the beach, on a small stretch of smooth sand, surrounded by large rocks. The violent storm must have blown itself out, for the sky was now a deep, calm blue, and the air was clean.

He looked down at the blanket covering him, and found it to be a woven mat—not the smooth reed mats used for floor covering that he was accustomed to, but a thick, scratchy mat woven of some hairy fiber. The material against his skin felt scratchy as well. Pulling aside his blanket, he saw that his wet clothes had been taken off, and that he was wearing an undergarment of an extremely coarse cloth, and over it a tunic of fur, with the fur side against his skin. The very unfamiliarity of the articles sent a thrill of alarm rushing through him.

He looked sharply at Zenta, and noticed for the first time that his friend was dressed in a similarly exotic manner, except that the furry garment turned out to be a cloak, not a tunic as he had thought at first. On his feet, Zenta wore not their own straw boots, but boots made of the skin of some animal. What made Matsuzo sit up abruptly,

9

however, was not the sight of Zenta's fantastical costume.

Behind his friend stood three men, and they were the strangest that he had ever seen. It was not just their clothes, which were similar to what Zenta was wearing. It was their faces.

Actually, Matsuzo had seen men in the capital city with features just as strange: Europeans from across the sea. He and Zenta had even become friendly with one of them, a Portuguese soldier of fortune called Pedro. Like Pedro, these men standing silently behind Zenta had deep-set, round eyes fringed by long, curly lashes. Could their little boat have drifted all the way across the sea to the land of Portugal? But this was not possible. He remembered Pedro saying that it had taken him the greater part of a year to sail from his country. Their boat had been adrift for little more than a week.

Moreover, Europeans had very long noses, which had earned them the name of Long-Nosed Devils. These men here had normal noses, with the bridges only a little higher than that of the average Japanese. The thing that struck Matsuzo the most about these men was their hairiness: They were the hairiest people he had ever seen. All three men had a mop of thick black hair, slightly curly and worn loose down to their shoulders. Full beards and mustaches covered the lower part of their faces, and bushy eyebrows hung over their strange, round eyes. The small portion of their faces that was visible showed their skin to be quite fair.

Matsuzo knew from his acquaintance with Europeans that appearance was not everything. Strange-looking or not, were these people friends or enemies? Could they even communicate with them? He glanced at Zenta, seeking a clue from his friend's expression.

And the expression on Zenta's face was an unexpected one. He seemed, of all things, to be embarrassed. He held out a small wooden bowl containing some thick, dark-colored gruel. "If you feel better now, how about trying some of this? It's not bad."

Matsuzo suddenly discovered that he was ravenous. Taking the bowl with shaky hands, he raised it to his lips and took a sip. Zenta was right. The gruel was not bad. It reminded him of a thick soup made of sweet potatoes, which he had loved as a child. The color of this gruel was much darker, however, and it had an unfamiliar earthy flavor. But he was much too hungry to care, and finished the bowl in a few quick slurps. Then he looked up at the three silent strangers and, in gratitude, tried a smile. They simply looked at him.

"They are friendly, aren't they, these people?" Matsuzo asked uneasily.

Zenta turned around and looked at the three men. Instantly they backed away, threw themselves on the ground, and began bowing frantically.

Zenta's expression of embarrassment returned. "They seem to think I'm some sort of god," he muttered.

Matsuzo stared at his friend. Zenta had always been lean, but now he was gaunt from starvation. Hollow-cheeked, unshaven, uncombed, and dressed in his borrowed clothes, Zenta looked anything but godlike.

"How about persuading them to send us back to the land of the gods, then?" asked Matsuzo, when he found his voice again.

"A good idea," agreed Zenta. "All I have to do is find some way to communicate with them."

One of the men rose to his feet and, still with head bowed humbly, made waving motions with his hands. His two companions rose as well and made similar motions.

"Well, that's easy to understand," Matsuzo said. "It's pretty clear that they want us to go with them. Shall we?"

Zenta grinned ruefully. "We don't have much choice."

Matsuzo struggled up from the ground. As he put his weight on his right foot, he felt a burning pain on his leg. Wincing, he lifted the edge of his fur cloak and looked at his calf: A large patch of skin had been scraped off, laying open the raw flesh beneath. It had probably happened when their boat had hit the rocks.

"That looks ugly," Zenta said, peering at the raw patch. "I hope it doesn't turn poisonous."

Their guides looked at Matsuzo's calf, muttered something, and made more waving motions.

Matsuzo sighed. "We'd better go. Maybe these people can find something to put on my leg." He folded his coarse blanket and handed it to one of the men. They might revere Zenta, but he didn't know how *he* was regarded, and it was always better to be polite.

Apparently Matsuzo's gesture was appreciated, for the man who received the blanket smiled at him. The others began to gather various objects strewn on the beach, and Matsuzo noticed that a number of things from their boat had been recovered, including the two bows and remaining arrows. They even had the dead sea gull. The men handled the bows very carefully, Matsuzo noticed.

Zenta followed his glance. "I have the impression it was my shooting with the bow that got them excited," he said.

"It was a good piece of shooting," admitted Matsuzo. "But there was nothing *supernatural* about it. Why should it have had such an effect?"

Zenta sighed. "We may never find out, unless we learn some of their language."

Even without the benefit of language, however, they could see that the three strangers showed unmistakable signs of impatience. Finally they said something in their own tongue and pointed. Again, spoken language seemed unnecessary.

"I think the sun is going to set pretty soon," said Zenta, "and they want us to start moving. It will be freezing cold as soon as it gets dark." He added dryly, "Even a god had better not keep his guides waiting."

The two samurai straightened their unfamiliar clothes as well as they could, and tightened their sashes, which resembled ropes. Matsuzo felt the gritty salt on his skin and yearned for a long, hot bath. But as he followed their guides, he began to suspect that getting a bath might not be easy. A ripe kind of smell came from the three strangers.

They followed a trail that climbed steadily from the shore, and Matsuzo found it almost impossible to keep up. The pain in his leg became more fierce with every step, and the path was treacherous with ice. Even Zenta, climbing in front of him, walked without his usual energy. It was nearly spring when they left Mutsu, but winter seemed to be lingering longer here, for they could see snow around them.

In spite of his misery, Matsuzo could not help noticing that many of the trees around them were unfamiliar. He was particularly struck by some trees with white-colored bark. Tall, bare, and slen-der, they looked ghostly. Suddenly he faltered, intensely aware of the fact that he was far from home and surrounded by strangers whose language he couldn't begin to understand.

Zenta glanced back, and Matsuzo saw that his friend didn't seem at all depressed by the thought of being in a strange land. On the contrary, he looked excited. As the pain in his leg increased, Matsuzo began to feel a rising resentment. It was Zenta's actions that had got them here. If only he hadn't insulted the powerful official whose son he was coaching in swordsmanship. The boy had the lumpish look of a badly kneaded rice cake, and he bullied younger boys unmercifully. But did Zenta have to point this out to the doting father?

Seven years younger than Zenta, Matsuzo had been accepted by the other man as a pupil, al-though nothing formal had been said. There were times when Zenta treated him as a younger brother.

At other times, it seemed that Matsuzo was the level-headed one. Zenta was occasionally subject to spells of brooding, and these led him to acts of rashness verging on self-destruction. The way he had offended the powerful official in Mutsu was simply the latest example. Matsuzo knew that his own good sense and the help of their friends had saved them.

And now they had been blown to this remote northern land and they might never see their own country again. Not being able to speak the local language, they might as well be deaf and dumb. Matsuzo was pierced by a pang of homesickness and groaned aloud.

"Is your leg paining you?" Zenta asked, looking concerned.

Matsuzo took a deep breath. "My leg is all right. I'm just a little winded from the climb." The two of them should consider themselves lucky to be alive, he thought. If it were not for these strangers, they would have drowned, or died from exposure in their wet clothes.

Their guides stopped. One of the three men, who seemed to be the leader, spoke briefly to his two companions. Then he stooped and thrust his arms carefully into the scrub bamboo by the side of the trail. He brought out an object that looked like a small bow, with a very short arrow attached to it by a string. Holding the bow in his hand, he motioned the others to proceed. After they had all passed, the man carefully put the bow back into the bushes. They could hear the rustle of the broad bamboo leaves as he fixed the bow in place again.

"That's a very strange bow," said Matsuzo, looking back. "He seems to be setting a trap across the trail. I wonder how he does that?"

"Where have I seen a bow like that before?" murmured Zenta, also looking back curiously. "I remember now: It's a spring bow. The arrow can be set to fire when someone trips the cord." He looked thoughtful. "Maybe this is how these people defend their territory."

But Matsuzo was losing interest even in the spring bow. His leg seemed to be on fire, and he was so tired that his head was beginning to swim. What would happen if he just lay down on the ground? Would these people carry him, or would they just abandon him?

Stumbling along in a daze, Matsuzo lost track of time. They could have been walking for days. Their arrival took him by surprise, and he nearly bumped into Zenta when they finally stopped walking. The leader of the guides called out, and someone answered from a distance.

Raising his head, Matsuzo saw that they had arrived at a clearing. The sun had not set. That meant that they couldn't have been hiking very long, after all. There was a house in the clearing, and in the mellow afternoon light, Matsuzo could see two men standing by the entrance. Close to the house, which had a snow-covered thatched roof, there were some smaller sheds.

One of these sheds, the one closest to the main house, appeared to be an enclosure with bars made of stout pieces of wood. As they approached the house, Matsuzo wondered in a panic if the enclosure might be an open-air prison, intended for strangers like himself and Zenta. When they reached the enclosure, however, he saw that it was already occupied—by a dark-brown, furry animal about the size of a large dog. But its legs did not look right for a dog. When the animal sat up, Matsuzo saw to his utter amazement that it was a bear cub.

The leading guide spoke to the two men standing in front of the house. The elder of the two men had grizzled hair and beard, while the other one, much younger, had only the fuzzy beginning of a beard.

The guide appeared from his gestures to be describing the shipwreck. He also made a motion imitating the stretching of a bow. At that, the two men in front of the house both turned and looked keenly at Zenta. Another burst of dialogue followed. After the exchange had gone on for what seemed like a long time, the younger man finally approached the two samurai. He smiled, and when he spoke, Matsuzo nearly broke out crying with joy.

For the man spoke in his own language—in Japanese.

TWO

The young man spoke Japanese with a heavy accent, but he was perfectly understandable. "My brother Ashiri and his friends believe that you are the god Okikumuri," he told Zenta. "You used the long bow that he is supposed to use, and when you shot an arrow into the sky, you called forth a storm."

He seemed friendly enough, but his deep, round eyes showed very little awe. "*I* believe, on the other hand, that you are a mortal, and that you and your friend are either castaways from your mainland or outcasts from the Japanese settlement down the river."

Zenta heard Matsuzo gasp behind him and

knew that his friend was elated on hearing that a settlement of their own people was close by. It was welcome news, but it did not mean their troubles were over. For all they knew, these people might be hostile to the Japanese. If Zenta confessed to being only a mortal, their rescuers might throw the two of them back into the sea as so much flotsam.

Should he pretend to be a god, then? In his twenty-five turbulent years of life, Zenta had been forced to put on many disguises. He had acted the role of a farmer, a priest, an idiot, and even an old hag. But he didn't think he could sustain the role of a god. Okikumuri—was that the name of the god? What was he supposed to be able to do, besides calling forth storms?

Honesty was the safest, in fact the only, course. "You are right," admitted Zenta. "We are no gods, but Japanese mortals, as you suspected. However, we know nothing about the Japanese settlement down the river here. In fact we don't even know what country this is, or who rules it."

The young man looked thoughtful. "So you are castaways, then."

Zenta nodded. "Our boat was blown to your shores after we lost our oar in a storm. We thought at first that we might land in China. But this is in the wrong direction."

"You are on the southern coast of the island of Ezo," the young man told Zenta.

Ezo! Zenta tried to remember what he had heard about this large, northern island. It was inhabited by a race of people called Ainus, and these men were undoubtedly members of that race. Zenta remembered now that the Ainus had always been described as being unusually hairy.

"Ezo," Matsuzo echoed softly. "Then there's some hope of getting home, after all! We're separated from the mainland only by the Tsugaru Straits."

Zenta looked curiously at the Ainu men before him. They were little better than savages, according to some accounts, and had no notions of metalworking, pottery, agriculture, and other trappings of civilization. And yet the Ainus he had met so far appeared to have a natural dignity. Zenta would certainly not describe them as savages.

Meanwhile the young speaker of Japanese and the three men from the beach seemed to be engaged in a heated argument. Suddenly the grizzled elder man barked out a command. They all turned and stared at the two samurai. Zenta tried to look impassive.

Sensing a movement behind him, he spun around and saw that Matsuzo had put his hand on the hilt of his sword. "No," Zenta said to him quickly. "We owe these people our lives, and we must not lift our hands against them!"

The young Ainu smiled, and his face showed approval. "I'm very glad you said that. You could have killed some of us here, perhaps all of us, for I've already seen demonstrations of your deadly swords. But if you had, you would not have lived to reach your countrymen afterward. Our friends would see to that."

Zenta could believe him. He remembered the little spring bow in the forest. How many other traps had they set? "What do you intend to do with us?" he asked.

"We have not yet decided," said the young Ainu. "A general council of our people must be called and the matter thoroughly discussed. But for now, please enter our home and accept some food and rest."

For the moment food and rest were what Zenta wanted more than anything else. He looked back at Matsuzo, who nodded agreement. His companion must have realized also that being reunited with their own people was impossible at present. Rest was what he needed, from the looks of him.

Zenta bowed gravely to their young host. "Thank you. My name is Konishi Zenta, and I gratefully accept your hospitality."

Matsuzo bowed as well. "My name is Ishihara Matsuzo. I'm glad to receive your goodwill."

The words were spoken a little grudgingly. The young Ainu who had invited them smiled. Again his eyes twinkled, and Zenta found himself warming to him. There was intelligence here. "My name is Tonkuru," he said, "and this is my father, the headman. My brother, Ashiri, and his friends are the ones who rescued you from the sea and brought you here."

The grizzled older man bowed gravely and uttered a few words in his own language. Again, Zenta was impressed by his grace and dignity. He was the headman, according to his son Tonkuru. Headman of what?

The headman spoke to his elder son, Ashiri, and the other two guides. Apparently he was dismissing them, for they picked up their gear and prepared to leave. But Ashiri looked back for a moment and frowned at the two samurai. Zenta guessed that Ashiri was unhappy about leaving Tonkuru and the headman alone in the company of two armed, potentially dangerous strangers.

"Please enter our house," Tonkuru invited the two Japanese.

Although Tonkuru was the youngest of the men they had met so far, he seemed to be the one who was taking most of the initiative. Zenta resolved to find the explanation for this.

Meanwhile, he was glad to receive refreshments in any form, and a warm, sheltered place in which to sleep. Following their hosts, the two Japanese passed through a shedlike structure and entered their first Ainu dwelling.

Zenta first noticed the smell. It was a smell that would grow very familiar to him in the coming days, so familiar that he would hardly notice it after a while. The scent of fish—dried fish and fish oil—predominated. Added to that was the smell of animal fat, drying kelp, herbs—some familiar, some unfamiliar—and over everything, the smell of unwashed human bodies. Behind him Zenta heard Matsuzo's steps falter and recoil. His young friend was extremely fastidious about personal grooming.

But after more than a week adrift in a boat, the two samurai themselves were hardly immaculate. Zenta followed his hosts into the interior and looked around.

At first it was too dark for him to see much. The last rays of the sun barely reached the windows, and the only other light came from the wood fire in a sunken fireplace. As his eyes gradually adjusted to the dimness, he saw that they were in a one-room house, with a fire pit in the middle.

In the corner to his right Zenta saw what looked like tools and weapons: short bows, spears, nets. To his left he saw a small loom, a mortar and pestle, wooden bowls, and other household utensils. He also saw something shiny that looked like lacquer ware. To his amazement, he recognized a tier of Japanese lacquered dishes.

At the sight of these familiar objects, Zenta felt his throat tighten. So far he had found this exotic new land an exciting adventure, but now he too felt an unexpected yearning for the familiar.

"You've noticed our lacquered dishes, have you?" said Tonkuru. He had not missed Zenta's glance. "Some of our people call these things 'treasures,' and we get them from trading with your countrymen. That small dish there, for instance, cost us two deerskins."

His expression was sardonic, even bitter. It was clear that Tonkuru himself did not consider the lacquer ware valuable and felt that his people had been cheated in the trade. The young Ainu was not as friendly toward the Japanese as Zenta had thought.

"Please sit," invited Tonkuru, indicating some reed mats close to the fire pit. "We will try to offer you food that won't offend your tastes too much."

There was a rustle, and two women whom Zenta had not noticed earlier moved forward from a dark corner to the fire pit. They held pieces of pink-fleshed salmon skewered on slender sticks, which they arranged over the fire. Almost immediately, the fat from the fish dripped into the fire, and a mouth-watering aroma rose from the pit.

Zenta swallowed the saliva in his mouth. Trying to control his hunger, he tore his eyes from the sizzling pieces of fish and turned to look at the two women. They were now ladling a grayish mush into wooden bowls.

The smaller figure stole a look at him, and Zenta saw big, round eyes, bright with intelligence. She suddenly grinned at him, with a hint of the same sardonic humor as Tonkuru's. From the likeness, Zenta suspected that Tonkuru and the girl were brother and sister. How old was she? It's always hard to judge the age of people belonging to a different race, but from her teeth and the size of her slender wrists, he guessed her age to be around ten or eleven.

Then the older woman turned her face to the light, and he received a shock. Like all the Ainu people he had met so far, she had deep-set, round eyes and fair skin, but these features he hardly noticed. He stared at her mouth: a great black gash of a mouth that stretched almost from ear to ear.

Then the woman said something to the girl, and

Zenta realized that the black streak was not her open mouth, but something painted across her lips and chin, and it was dark blue, not black.

"This is my mother," said Tonkuru's voice. "And the little girl is my sister Mopi."

Zenta blushed, realizing that he had been caught staring. He bowed his head to the woman and tried not to look at the grotesque slash across her mouth. Next to him, Matsuzo swallowed audibly and imitated Zenta's bow.

"Perhaps you are wondering about the blue tattoo on my mother's face," said Tonkuru. His keen eyes had not missed their reaction. "Our women do it to make themselves more beautiful. Their hands and arms are tattooed as well."

Zenta had seen a pattern on the woman's arms, and he had assumed that she was wearing cloth sleeves. Now he saw that her lower arms were bare but tattooed. His glance went involuntarily to the face of the little girl, Mopi. She was a winsome creature, round eyes and all, and he was glad she had no disfiguring tattoos. He cleared his throat. "Do all the women have to have the tattooing done?"

"As soon as they reach maturity, which is around the age of seventeen," answered Tonkuru. "A girl is considered ready for marriage when her tattooing is completed."

Matsuzo made a sound. He was also looking regretfully at Mopi.

Tonkuru smiled wryly. "You don't find the custom attractive? How about Japanese women? Do they do anything to their faces?"

Zenta was silenced, for he knew that Japanese married women, especially among the upper classes, often plucked out all their eyebrows and dyed their teeth black.

Fortunately, he was saved from having to answer when the hot food was served, and he could begin eating. In addition to the salmon on skewers, they had stewed fern tips and bowls of a boiled grain, nutty in flavor. Tonkuru told the two guests that it was bamboo seeds. Zenta found it a delicious meal, if unfamiliar in taste and texture. The food would certainly have been improved by a dash of soy sauce, but hunger took the place of seasoning.

Zenta followed the example of his hosts and ate the fish right off the skewers, while using his fingers on the vegetables. He was amused to see that Matsuzo broke his wooden skewers in two. Since the sticks were slightly bent, what he had was a pair of bowlegged chopsticks. Matsuzo picked up a piece of stewed fern, which promptly slipped and fell back into his bowl.

A giggle burst from Mopi, who had been watching

the actions of the young samurai with avid interest. Her mother made a shushing noise, and Mopi stifled her giggling with her hands, but the corners of her eyes still crinkled with mirth.

Matsuzo blushed. He turned one of the two sticks around in his hand, so that they now curved in parallel arcs instead of being bowlegged. Again he picked up a piece of fern. Again it plopped back. Mopi bent over and shook with suppressed laughter, and even her parents had to hide smiles. Sighing, Matsuzo put down his makeshift chopsticks and resorted to using his fingers.

After satisfying the worst of his hunger, Zenta could no longer keep back some of his urgent questions. "Can you tell me how you happen to speak our language so well?" he asked Tonkuru.

"How kind of you to say that I speak it well," said Tonkuru, smiling.

"I speak, too," said little Mopi.

Tonkuru laughed aloud, obviously enjoying the surprise of the guests. "I learned to speak from trading with the Japanese settlement, and then I taught my sister a few words. She learns very fast."

Looking at the girl's bright, intelligent eyes, Zenta could well believe that she was a fast learner. He turned back to Tonkuru. "Your accent is very good. You must have received some special coaching."

Tonkuru's smile faded. "Yes, I did," he said heavily, and didn't elaborate.

Matsuzo broke the silence. "How large is the Japanese settlement? Has it been there long?"

"I'm not sure when they first arrived," replied Tonkuru. "As far as my father knows, the settlement was already there at the time of *his* father. At first the Japanese had little to do with us, and most of the men spent their time on the sea, fishing. But in recent years they've started to raise crops, and they are spending more time farming than fishing. Now they get most of their salmon from us, as well as furs and wood products. In return, we get some of the grains they raise, like millet, as well as utensils, metal tools, and cloth. Some of our women began to covet Japanese cloth, since it's so much softer than our own, which is woven from the inner bark of elm trees."

"Toys, too!" Mopi suddenly cried. She jumped to her feet, ran to a corner of the room, and returned with something tenderly cradled in her arms. It was a Japanese doll, dressed in a silk brocade kimono.

Tonkuru's face darkened at the sight of the doll, and he barked a few curt words at his sister. She listened with lowered head and trembling lips. Then slowly she put the doll back in the corner.

Tonkuru might speak good Japanese and he

31

might be friendly toward the two castaways, but he was clearly displeased by the way his sister and others of his people delighted in Japanese goods.

The Japanese settlement was evidently a very sensitive topic. Zenta now recalled that the settlers in Ezo were mostly followers of a family called Matsumae. With Japan torn apart by civil wars, many families had been dispossessed, and some had emigrated to the northern island. Perhaps some of the men were ronin like himself and Matsuzo, samurai without masters.

"Have your relations with the Japanese been peaceful?" he asked cautiously. His future and safety, and Matsuzo's as well, depended on the answer.

To his relief, Tonkuru answered easily. "Oh, yes. My father, the headman, has always urged the people of this *kotan* to live in peace with the settlers."

"What is a kotan?" asked Matsuzo.

Tonkuru hesitated. "There is no word in your language that corresponds exactly to kotan. It's not quite as big as a village. A kotan consists of a group of families who live close together and cooperate in hunting and fishing. Our kotan, for instance, consists of this household, the household of my uncles, and that of my elder brother. Most important of all, we perform certain rituals

together, like the Salmon Ceremony, in lat
mer, and the Bear Ceremony, which wi
place in just a few days."

Matsuzo looked enthralled. "Bear Ceremony? Is
that why you have that bear cub outside? And the
Salmon Ceremony? What—"

Zenta knew that they could spend the whole
evening, and many subsequent evenings, discussing the customs of the Ainu people. But there
was one question that he wanted to ask immediately. "The headman makes most of the decisions,
then?"

"When something arises, the headman makes
suggestions and gives advice," said Tonkuru. "The
rest of the kotan gather to discuss the matter, but
most often follow his lead."

"And who will succeed your father as headman?" asked Zenta. He could guess what the
answer would be.

And he was right. "I shall be the next headman," replied Tonkuru. "According to the custom
of our kotan, the youngest son of the headman is
trained to be his successor."

Matsuzo's jaw dropped. "The *youngest* son? Not
the *eldest*?"

Tonkuru's bushy brows rose. "Is it the custom of
your people always to choose the eldest son?"

Matsuzo looked nonplussed. "Well, we try to

choose the son with the greatest experience, and that's usually the eldest one. Of course, if he turns out to be ineligible for some reason, we go on to the next one."

Zenta thought he could guess why the youngest son was chosen. "By the time the headman becomes too old, his eldest son would be somewhat along in years as well, whereas the youngest boy would have many more prime years left. Is that right?"

Tonkuru beamed. "Exactly. I'm a green and inexperienced youth, but fortunately my father still has many active years left to him. By the time he is ready to retire, I shall be mature, but still young enough to be headman for a number of years yet."

He turned to his father and smiled. The headman smiled back with obvious pride and love. He seemed to understand some of the exchange between his son and the Japanese guests.

It sounds like a very practical system, thought Zenta. Then he remembered the face of Tonkuru's elder brother, Ashiri, who had been the leader among the three guides. It was the face of a stubborn man. "How does your elder brother feel about following the leadership of a younger brother?" he asked Tonkuru.

"He accepts the system," Tonkuru said calmly. "After all, it has been the custom of our kotan for as long as we remember. But speaking of my elder brother reminds me: I've asked Ashiri to be your host for the time being."

Zenta tried to conceal his dismay at the arrangement. After the companionship of Tonkuru and that of his little sister, Mopi, he didn't look forward to spending the night with Ashiri's family, who didn't speak Japanese. Matsuzo looked equally unenthusiastic at the prospect before them. But they were hardly in a position to complain.

Tonkuru was already rising. "Let me take you to Ashiri's house. You must be tired and in need of your bed."

Mopi jumped up. "I go too."

There was nothing to do but follow, and the two samurai rose. Matsuzo winced as he put his weight on his right leg.

"Did you hurt your leg?" asked Tonkuru.

Matsuzo lifted his tunic. On his calf a streaky scab was forming over the raw flesh, but the leg looked puffy and sore.

A hiss came from the headman's wife, and she immediately issued orders to her daughter. The girl hurried back with some water in a wooden bowl and a wad of spongy-looking material, which turned out to be moss.

Matsuzo was made to sit down again, and the headman's wife began to wash the scrape. Zenta could see from his friend's tightly clenched teeth that the washing was painful. He was also uneasy about the unwholesome-looking wad of brown moss used to cleanse the wound. But at least this was better than not doing anything at all to the wound—he hoped. Short of finding their way to the Japanese settlement, there was nothing they could do.

After she had wiped Matsuzo's leg, the head-man's wife covered the scrape with some pungent black ointment. As the ointment touched the raw flesh, a yelp escaped Matsuzo.

Mopi squeezed his hand and made soothing noises. "It hurts, but it's good," she told the young samurai. "I cut my hand, and the black medicine helped."

Matsuzo managed a smile and squeezed her hand back. The headman's wife, after applying the black ointment, wrapped the scraped leg with some soft binding that seemed to be made of tree bark. She tied it in place with twine. Matsuzo bore the bandaging stoically, and when the headman's wife had finished, he rose and thanked her.

The two Japanese then bowed to the headman. The headman nodded his head gravely, and his wife smiled shyly. Zenta found that he could now look at the blue tattoo around her mouth without wincing.

As soon as Mopi went outside, she went to the cage containing the bear cub and crooned to it. There was a wooden box near the cage containing some acorns and dried berries. Mopi scooped up a handful of the berries and reached into the cage to place them in front of the cub, which picked them up and unhurriedly munched, letting the red juice dribble down its chin. Mopi laughed delightedly.

Matsuzo smiled. "Your friend? This bear cub?"

"Friend?" Mopi tried out the word. "Not friend. Bear is . . ." She groped unsuccessfully for the right word, and finally just shook her head.

Matsuzo picked up a handful of berries and placed them in front of the bear cub. It stared at him for a moment and suddenly growled. He jumped hurriedly back. Mopi laughed.

"This bear cub is our guest, but it is not really tame," warned Tonkuru. "Be careful not to get too close."

"I won't," Matsuzo promised fervently.

Tonkuru started off down the path leading into the woods. Before the two samurai could take more than a couple of steps, they heard the bear cub growl right behind their backs. They gasped and whirled around—and found Mopi nearly doubled up laughing. Then she straightened and uttered a few more growls for good measure.

"The little imp!" muttered Matsuzo, embarrassed.

Dusk was beginning to change into night, and they had little time to waste. Tonkuru walked quickly and confidently, with Mopi tripping lightly behind him. Zenta tried to keep up, but remembering the spring bow in the bushes he had seen earlier, he found himself treading cautiously. Furthermore, he was not quite used to his deerskin boots and found the ground extremely treacherous, now that the ice had hardened in the cold air.

Matsuzo lagged even farther behind, and Zenta became worried. "How is your leg? Is it worse?"

Matsuzo limped forward a few steps. "It burns, but I can walk on it."

Nevertheless the Ainus had to stop several times and wait for the two men. Fortunately they did not have far to go.

They came to another clearing, a smaller one, and saw a house similar in structure to that of Tonkuru and his parents. As they approached the house, Zenta saw that it also had a wooden cage near the entrance, with a bear cub inside. Mopi went up to the cage and crooned to the bear, but quickly moved back when her elder brother, Ashiri, came out of the house.

Ashiri and Tonkuru exchanged a few words. The younger brother turned to the two samurai. "Ashiri says he is happy to have you as his guests and hopes that you will find his house comfortable."

Looking at the brooding face of the elder brother, Zenta wondered if Tonkuru's translation of his brother's words had been completely accurate. Ashiri had thought that Zenta was a god. Having found out his mistake, he might feel somewhat foolish. Perhaps he harbored some resentment toward the two strangers who had caused the misunderstanding.

There was nothing to do, however, but to accept the hospitality, even if it was grudgingly given. Tonkuru was already turning away and pulling the reluctant Mopi after him. "Sleep well," he said to the two Japanese.

Following Ashiri into his house, Zenta found himself in a room similar to the one in the headman's home. It also contained a sunken fireplace, hunting and fishing gear, cooking utensils, and a loom. Here, too, he saw a shelf of Japanese objects, which Tonkuru had contemptuously called "treasures." Besides lacquer dishes, Zenta noticed some ceramic ware: a few clay bowls and a blue-and-white china jar.

Ashiri's wife, a slender young woman, was spreading out some sleeping mats on a low wooden platform. When she looked around, Zenta was prepared this time for the wide blue tattoo across her mouth. Ashiri pointed to her and said curtly, "Okera." She looked briefly at the strangers and turned her head away, but not before Zenta caught a smile lurking at the corner of her mouth.

Ashiri indicated the two mats. It was clear that the guests were being shown their sleeping places. Okera, his wife, retired to a corner of the room, which had been partitioned off by some hanging screens made of reeds.

Zenta sank down on one of the mats. It was not particularly soft, but it was fresh-smelling and dry. He had had to sleep on the bare ground often enough, and found the sleeping arrangement in Ashiri's house pleasant by comparison. The hard part was falling asleep under the eyes of such a reluctant host.

But Zenta felt almost dizzy with fatigue. Matsuzo was already lying on his mat with his eyes closed. Zenta decided to follow his example. Murmuring some words, which he hoped his hosts would correctly interpret as thanks, Zenta stretched out on his mat and spread his fur cape up to his chin as a cover. Just before he fell asleep, he wondered when the Ainus would be trading next with the Japanese settlers. He hoped it would be very soon.

THREE

Matsuzo opened his eyes to near darkness. He saw that only a dim, milky light reached the window facing east, and he estimated the time to be well before dawn. What had awakened him? He looked at Zenta's sleeping mat and saw that it was empty. Sitting up abruptly, he turned his eyes toward the entrance. The woven grass screen over the door had been lifted aside.

Looking around the room again, Matsuzo noticed that the screens in front of the sleeping area for Ashiri and his wife were pushed aside, and their sleeping mats were empty. He himself was the last one up. He flung aside his fur cape and got to his feet. The blood rushed into his sore leg like a bolt of lightning, and he groaned aloud.

Then he bit his lip, afraid that he had been overheard; it would be too humiliating. But no one was there.

Despite his aching leg he had slept soundly, without interruption. Now he felt refreshed and very hungry. He hoped that whatever had roused his hosts at this early predawn hour, it had something to do with food.

He limped to the front entrance, and outside he found Ashiri and Zenta bent over something on the ground. The Ainu was using a piece of vine to tie a large hook to a wooden shaft. His sinewy fingers, covered with black hair, were strong and deft. In a few minutes he had the hook securely fastened, and the result was a form of harpoon.

At Matsuzo's approach, Zenta looked up. "Good morning. So you're finally up. I don't have to ask if you slept well. How is the leg?"

"I've been afraid to look," admitted Matsuzo. "But at least it doesn't hurt more than before."

He turned and greeted Ashiri. The Ainu looked briefly at him and muttered a reply, but his face was less surly. He hefted the harpoonlike spear and seemed satisfied with its balance.

It was still well before dawn, and Matsuzo had to peer hard at the spearhead to realize that it was made of iron. "Do these people use iron weapons? I thought they still used stone tools. And the arrowhead of the spring bow we saw was made of bamboo."

"I saw other iron tools in the house," said Zenta. He had evidently had time to look around this morning. "There were some knives made of steel, and the hook for hanging cooking pots over the fire pit was made of iron as well. They could have obtained the implements from trading with the Japanese settlement."

Matsuzo looked at Ashiri's hooked spearhead. "This is a pretty vicious-looking weapon."

The Ainu hefted his spear, pointed toward a footpath, and made beckoning motions.

"Do you know what he's planning to do?" Matsuzo asked Zenta. "I hope it won't take long, because I'm starved."

"Then you'll be glad to know that he's planning to spear some fish," replied Zenta. "Unless I've misunderstood his sign language."

"*Spear* fish?" asked Matsuzo. "I have to see this to believe it!"

The two samurai followed the Ainu down a rapidly descending path—Matsuzo with some difficulty—and soon they heard the sound of running water. Dawn was on the point of breaking when they approached the river—a stream, actually; they could see where it branched off from the main body of the river a little way up. The shallows near the banks were still frozen, but water was running in the middle of the stream. By the time they reached it, the first rays of the sun touched and gilded the surface of the water.

Ashiri's feet crunched into the ice as he stepped into the stream and waded to the middle. Then, with his hand holding the spear at his shoulder, he stood absolutely still and stared intently into the water.

The two Japanese stepped into the stream as well. Matsuzo cried out at the cold, which he could feel even through his thick waterproof boots. He closed his mouth as the Ainu turned and glared at him. After a minute his feet began to ache, but he soon forgot the pain when he was able to make out moving shapes in the water. Fish—he saw whole schools of fish swimming rapidly past his feet.

There was a splash. The Ainu's spear had descended. It came up from the water with a wriggling fish at the end of it. He grinned at his two watchers and deposited the fish on the bank, obviously enjoying their astonishment and admiration. The fish flapped a few times and lay still. With his spear raised again, the Ainu went back to staring down into the water.

Matsuzo slowly released his breath. *If Ashiri decides to use his spear on human beings as well as on fish, he will be a powerful fighter,* he thought.

There was another splash, but this time Ashiri's spear came up empty. He instantly went back to his watchful stance. Seconds later, the spear struck into the water again, and another flapping fish was deposited on the bank.

"Marvelous," murmured Zenta. The Ainu heard and smiled. He needed no common language to hear the admiration in Zenta's voice.

A faint rustle came from the tall, white trees on the other side of the stream. Instantly, the three men jerked to attention. In the morning sun the white trunks looked pink, but behind the trunks Matsuzo caught a glimpse of a color that did not belong in these woods. He saw a flutter of something light blue, the blue of Japanese dyed cloth. And that meant that a countryman of his was at hand!

Without thinking of the consequences, Matsuzo called out. "Oi, over there! Are you from the settlement?"

A growl came from the Ainu. Gripping his spear tightly, he splashed across the stream toward the trees. Seeing the approach of disaster, Matsuzo started after Ashiri. He could not allow a fellow

Japanese to be hurt. An iron grip on his shoulder stopped him dead.

"We must not start a fight," said Zenta. His words were soft, but they demanded instant obedience.

Meanwhile the Ainu was just about to reach the opposite bank, but whoever was behind the trees had decided on flight. There was a louder rustle of bamboo, then some light footsteps. After that, only silence. Ashiri looked at the fleeing figure, than back to the two Japanese behind him. Slowly, he turned around and began recrossing the stream.

Matsuzo limped up to the bank of the stream and sat down next to the flapping fish. For a moment it had seemed that civilization was at hand. For a moment it had seemed that he and Zenta would join their countryman and together go to the settlement, where they could take a hot bath, sleep under quilts of soft cotton, and eat white rice in china bowls. He had to fight down a strong desire to weep, so keen was his disappointment.

Zenta sat down beside Matsuzo. "Don't be discouraged," he said. "The man knows that we're here now. Maybe they'll send someone who can guide us to the settlement. We'll talk to Tonkuru about it."

"The Ainus might not want to let us go," muttered Matsuzo. "Ashiri looks furious."

It was true. The Ainu, who had been on the verge of friendliness only a short while ago, was no longer smiling. He strung his fish on a piece of twine, shouldered his spear, and gestured to the two samurai and toward the path. The dark brooding was back on his face.

Matsuzo felt a hot streak of resentment. Why should they submit to the peremptory orders of the Ainu? They were being treated like prisoners—worse, herded like domestic animals. He started to make an angry retort, but bit it back. What was the use? The man wouldn't understand a word anyway.

Zenta touched him on the arm. "Let's go. Getting angry won't help matters."

"You'd think Ashiri would be glad to get rid of us," grumbled Matsuzo as they plodded glumly after the Ainu. "We're eating his food, occupying precious room in his house. What are they keeping us for?"

"I don't know," admitted Zenta. "It's a puzzle. If the Ainus really are friendly with the Japanese, there's no reason why they wouldn't just take us over to the settlement."

An uncomfortable thought occurred to Matsuzo. "If the Ainus consider the settlers enemies, they might be holding us here as hostages."

Zenta shook his head. "No, that can't be the reason. We have no connection with the settlers, and they didn't even know of our existence until now. We'd be of no value whatever as hostages. In fact we're of no value to anybody."

That was an even less comfortable thought. Still, these Ainus have taken the trouble to rescue us, feed us, lend us warm clothing, and lodge us with their own household, thought Matsuzo. They could have put us into a cage, like that bear cub.

At Ashiri's house, Okera had stirred up the embers of the fire in the pit. A steaming pot hung from a hook over the fire, and she was adding some chopped greens to it. An aromatic smell rose and filled the room. To the young ronin it was unfamiliar but not unpleasant.

When Okera saw her husband with his two fish, she spoke to him forcefully. She didn't raise her voice, but her manner was firm. It didn't need an understanding of the Ainu language for Matsuzo to guess that she found her husband's catch too meager. He himself had been impressed by Ashiri's skill, but evidently the woman had expected more than just two fish.

The Ainu seemed to be making excuses. Matsuzo was pretty sure that he was telling his wife how they had seen a Japanese man lurking behind the trees. The woman turned and glowered at the two samurai. As if we were to blame for interrupting the fishing, thought Matsuzo.

He was a little surprised at the Ainu for allowing his wife to speak out like that. With her blue-tattooed lips Okera was giving Ashiri a piece of her mind. Matsuzo thought wistfully of the modest demeanor of Japanese women.

At least Okera went about preparing breakfast efficiently. In a short time she had the fish cleaned, scaled, cut up, and put into the boiling pot. Soon she was ladling out the savory-smelling stew into wooden bowls. For eating the stew, each person had a small spoon made of white tree bark.

On the previous night Matsuzo had been too hungry and too tired to pay much attention to his eating utensils. This morning, he picked up his wooden bowl and observed that it was decorated on the outside with beautiful carving. There was a pattern of swirls and hooks, some reminding him of animals and some quite abstract. The bowl was beautiful—in a barbaric sort of way—and the stew was edible, though bland and saltless. Matsuzo sighed, unable to forget that he was trapped among an alien people.

Just as they were finishing the meal, they heard voices outside. Standing up, Ashiri peered out the window and greeted the newcomers. They were his brother, Tonkuru, and his sister, Mopi.

As soon as they entered, Mopi went over to Matsuzo and asked to see his leg. The young Japanese was slightly embarrassed. Baring his leg to a girl was not his normal mode of behavior— even to a young girl of an alien race.

Zenta smiled. "You'd better do it. Otherwise she will worry."

Trying not to blush, Matsuzo sat down and pulled up his coarse tunic. His leg was still wrapped in the bandage made of tree bark.

Mopi knelt down next to him and began to peel away the binding. Matsuzo, alarmed, began to stop her. But her fingers were deft and gentle. Even when she pulled off the part that was stuck to the wound, she hardly hurt him at all.

The wound was streaked with deep scratches and smeared with the black ointment. Matsuzo felt his leg throb with a pounding pulse, for laying it open to the air seemed to deepen the pain. The skin around the sore felt puffy and hot. Mopi clucked sympathetically as she looked.

Ashiri frowned and said something to his brother. "You must have been scratched by barnacles when your boat hit the rocks," said Tonkuru, translating. "They can cause a wound to turn ugly."

"That's not very reassuring," muttered Matsuzo. He was wondering whether the wound was turning ugly from the black ointment smeared on by the headman's wife.

Tonkuru seemed to sense his thoughts. "My mother's ointment should draw the poison from the wound. But you have to give it time to work."

Before Matsuzo could stop her, Mopi smeared more of the black ointment lavishly on his leg. She had carried a supply of the ointment and fresh bandages. Then, concentrating so hard that the tip of her tongue protruded, she wrapped his leg carefully and tied the bandage with twine. She looked up and beamed proudly at him when she was done.

Despite the red-hot pain from the ointment, Matsuzo couldn't help smiling back at her. "Do I have your august permission to arise from my sickbed?" he asked her, in the manner of a patient consulting an eminent physician.

She understood only half of his words, but she giggled at his grave manner. "Yes, you can get up. It's good to use your leg."

Ashiri began talking vehemently to his younger brother. Tonkuru's smile vanished, and all traces of friendliness disappeared. He turned to the two samurai. "Ashiri tells me that he saw a Japanese spying on him while he was fishing at the stream this morning. Do you know anything about this man?"

"How can we?" protested Matsuzo. "When we were shipwrecked on your coast, we didn't even know what country this was! And you've had us under your eyes ever since, so you know we didn't make contact with any of the people from the settlement."

"Is there any reason why you don't want us to communicate with people from the settlement?" Zenta asked the young Ainu. "Do you consider them your enemies?"

Tonkuru's lips were set grimly, but after a moment he sighed. "We did not consider the Japanese enemies—not when they first arrived in my great-grandfather's day and began to fish in our waters. Then they wanted land for cultivation, and we let them have it because we thought there was enough for everyone."

Ashiri and Okera were staring intently at Tonkuru as he addressed the two guests. How much Japanese did they understand? The woman's deep-set eyes seemed to glitter with strong feeling, and when Tonkuru had finished, she broke out into speech, accompanied by many vehement gestures.

"Okera says that she and her friends can no longer gather berries and roots on the patch of land at the foothills," Tonkuru said. "Apparently the Japanese are planning to cultivate millet and barley there."

Okera spoke again, sounding even angrier. "She said she used to go quite often to the settlement to trade deerskins," said Tonkuru. "But the last time she went, the Japanese were abusive. They were accusing our people of trying to frighten them off."

"And have you?" asked Zenta.

Tonkuru dropped his eyes. "They said something about a bear," he muttered. "Apparently there's a complaint about a bear terrorizing the settlers, and they blame it on us. Of course that's completely impossible."

A growl sounded behind Matsuzo, and he jumped. Then, hearing the giggling, he knew that he had been fooled—again.

"Mopi!" snapped Tonkuru. "Stop that! We're trying to talk seriously."

Zenta grinned. "I think she likes you," he told Matsuzo.

"Then she has a strange way of showing it," grumbled Matsuzo. Just when he had become grateful for the way she had tended his leg, she was turning back into a mischievous brat.

Zenta turned to the young Ainu. "Why don't you let us go to the settlement? Then we can find out what is behind the complaints about the bear. Perhaps we can end this misunderstanding and restore good relations between your people and the Japanese settlers."

Tonkuru did not reply immediately, and Matsuzo felt a chill. He had thought that this young Ainu was well disposed toward them, but now he realized that Tonkuru was not a man whose actions were governed by friendship—if indeed he was a real friend.

He and Zenta were quite alone. Even Mopi might just be amusing herself with them. She had bandaged his leg as she might bandage the limb of her doll. She had teased him as she might tease her captive bear.

Finally Tonkuru turned to the two Japanese. "Some of my people believe you may give away information about us to your countrymen. You have seen our tools and our weapons, and the arrangement of our houses. All these things could help the settlers mount an attack on our people."

"You saved our lives," Zenta said quietly. "You have given us hospitality. We would not betray you to the settlers."

"The decision on whether or not to release you is too important for our family to make," Tonkuru told the two Japanese. "Even my father, as headman, will have to consult our whole kotan, as well as other neighboring kotans."

Matsuzo felt his jaw ache and realized that he was clenching his teeth to keep back an angry outburst. How long were they to be kept prisoners? The two of them could fight their way out—they had escaped their enemies before. He was not afraid of the Ainus' spears and hidden bows!

"We will be having our Bear Festival in two days," continued Tonkuru. "During the festival our whole kotan will be present, and most of our neighbors will send representatives. My father says that the decision on your future will be made at that time."

FOUR

On the morning of the Bear Festival, Mopi took Matsuzo along with her on a round of all the houses in the kotan. In front of each one, she stopped by the bear cage and gave treats to the cub inside. She had chosen the biggest acorns and the best of the dried berries from her mother's store.

As he watched the girl handing out the treats, Matsuzo began to get over his own nervousness at being close to the caged animals. They seemed tame, and in their lumbering way they looked rather endearing. The one in front of the headman's house reminded him of a puppy he used to have, called Taro, who moved in the same clumsy manner and was also perpetually hungry. Mopi told him that each family had one of these cubs, and had been raising it for the Bear Festival.

Mopi had attached herself to the young samurai. "I have to see that your leg is getting well," she told him earnestly.

She took her duty as a nurse so seriously that Matsuzo found it hard to turn her away. It was true that she did a skillful job of washing and bandaging his wound. He only wished that she wouldn't smear it so thickly with the black ointment each time. The leg continued to pain him, and it remained red and swollen.

Although he tried not to let his worry show, Matsuzo wished more and more anxiously that a competent Japanese physician could look at his leg. But until they could escape from the Ainus and reach the Japanese settlement, he had to resign himself to the doubtful benefits of the foul-smelling black ointment.

At least one good thing resulted from Mopi's constant companionship during the last few days. Matsuzo and the girl began to exchange language lessons. Beside learning basic Ainu words for such things as *good*, *yes*, and *no*, he also learned the words for *hunter*, *bear*, *berries*, *acorns*, and *wild yam*. He now knew that the tree with the white trunk was called a "birch."

The girl told him proudly that her mother had taught her how to fold the bark of the birch tree into shallow dishes and dippers. She was also learning to weave cloth from the soft, fibrous inner bark of the elm tree.

She was becoming an accomplished cook, she said. "My brother say I make better yam mush than his wife, Okera."

Tonkuru overheard her boast. "Mopi! That's not true! You must not say that!"

"She's probably just exaggerating a little," said Matsuzo, feeling sorry for the girl, whose lips were trembling from her brother's rebuke.

"We Ainus feel very strongly about telling the truth," said Tonkuru. "I cannot let Mopi say something she knows is false."

It was hard to shake himself loose from Mopi, Matsuzo discovered. She left his side only to help her mother with various domestic tasks. Fortunately there were many of them, because all the womenfolk of the kotan were busily preparing for the festival. Okera was one of the busiest.

Matsuzo still found it surprising that Tonkuru, the younger son, had been chosen as successor to the headman, and already spoke with the authority and confidence of a future leader. He was not married, but if he had a wife, would she take precedence over Okera, Ashiri's wife? Matsuzo shook his head and decided to give up trying to understand the unfamiliar social structure of the Ainus.

With the help of Tonkuru and Mopi, he was beginning to get acquainted with some of their customs. He knew now that they considered lying to be detestable, even when it was for a good cause. He also learned that one of the things men dreaded most was a cursing wife. Okera, he was told by a grinning Tonkuru, was notorious for her sharp tongue.

While the womenfolk were busy preparing food and getting the headman's house ready, Tonkuru took the two Japanese to meet his uncle, who had just returned from a week-long hunting expedition with three other men. The men had spent the week at a rude hut in the mountains, and they hunted from early morning till the light failed. They came back with two deer well covered with winter fat.

The uncle, who was the elder brother of the headman, had long, grizzled hair and a beard reaching nearly to his waist. After his strenuous week, he still looked energetic and ready to enjoy the festivities to the fullest.

One thing immediately impressed Matsuzo: the great respect shown to the uncle by all the young men, who listened eagerly to his words and rushed to obey his commands. The respect was not due to his rank, since he was not the headman; his younger brother was. Perhaps the young men of the kotan looked up to him because of his outstanding skills as a hunter.

If this were a Japanese family, the uncle should by rights be the head of the household, thought Matsuzo. He wondered if the tough-looking, grizzled hunter ever resented being subordinate to his younger brother.

The two samurai were allowed to examine the bows used by the hunters. Beside the spring bow they had seen earlier, the hunters also used draw bows, both kinds considerably shorter than the bows carried by the Japanese.

The Ainu hunters were also very curious about the long Japanese bows, and that afternoon Zenta was asked to give demonstrations of his shooting. The Ainus set up pieces of white tree bark as targets, and after quickly shooting them down, Zenta asked Matsuzo to move the targets back, to twice the original distance.

The watchers began to talk excitedly. Matsuzo smiled to himself, for he suspected that most of the Ainus didn't believe Zenta could score a hit at this range. Ashiri and his two friends, who had seen him shoot down the sea gull, were the only ones who did not look skeptical.

A hush settled over the crowd as Zenta care-fully tested the breeze. He now took his time before drawing, and when he had the bow drawn to its fullest extent, he raised it, then lowered it, and gradually moved it up until it was at the height he wanted. Matsuzo recognized this man-nerism, which Zenta unconsciously adopted whenever he was concentrating most intently on his shooting.

There was a hiss and a thud. A scrap of white birch bark in the far distance disappeared, and an even greater hubbub broke out. Some of the women and children came running over to share the excitement. The superior range and power of the long bow had made a deep impression.

Tonkuru's uncle began to question his son closely. The young man was one of the three who had rescued the Japanese from the shipwreck, and he had seen Zenta shoot down the sea gull.

"*Your* archers are even more impressive," Zenta told the uncle, his words translated by Tonkuru. "I'm told some of them can even hit a fish swim-ming in the water. But to bring down a running deer, wouldn't you need more power?"

"No, because for shooting larger game, our arrows are poisoned," said Tonkuru before his uncle could reply. "We use the juice from a plant . . ." Tonkuru paused, and then confessed that he didn't know the Japanese name for the plant.

After he had described the plant, Zenta nodded. "I think I know the plant you mean. It's monkshood, or aconite. Our physicians use it in certain medicines, but it's a very dangerous drug."

Tonkuru's uncle evidently understood some of the exchange. He spoke sharply to the younger man, and Matsuzo guessed that the information about the poisoned arrows was not something he wanted to share with the two Japanese. Some of the other young men stirred angrily. They don't trust us, thought the young samurai.

They had been well treated, nevertheless. It would be ungrateful to complain when they had been rescued from drowning and freely given hospitality. Their host, Ashiri, might be somewhat sullen, but he was never deliberately rude. Okera was careful to serve the two guests first, and Matsuzo suspected that they were being given the choicest portions of the food. He wished that he could appreciate the food better, however, for he was getting very tired of gruel made from various roots, salmon, and smoked deer meat. He longed for a bowl of rice and some pickled radishes, just plain pickled radishes.

Perhaps there would be some special treats for the coming feast. Following Mopi, the two samurai made their way to the clearing in front of the headman's house, where the rituals were to take place. They saw that a rough circle had been marked out by a series of tripods made of wooden staffs. Resting in the crotch of each tripod was the skull of an animal or a bird.

There were also numerous short willow wands, with strips shaven back to form curls at the tops, which Mopi told him were called *inao*. Matsuzo gathered that they had some religious significance, probably similar to the white strips of folded paper and rice-straw ropes seen in the shrines of his own people. With the tripods and the wands, the clearing had a festive look.

A big crowd had already gathered, and when the two Japanese arrived, some of the chattering died down and eyes turned curiously in their direction. But it was hard to read the expressions in those bright, deep-set, round eyes. Matsuzo wondered what these Ainu people really felt about the presence of himself and Zenta at this important festival.

The ceremony began with the headman leading a circle of the men in chanting. The women and children sat in an outer circle, together with guests. These included not only the two Japanese, but also families from a couple of nearby kotans. To Matsuzo, the low-pitched chanting seemed to go on forever, and he found himself sinking into a daze. The droning sounded like the chant of a Buddhist priest, if one didn't listen too closely. By closing his eyes, he could imagine the silken robes of the priest, the curling roofs of the temple, the polished wooden floors . . . a refined, civilized world. . . .

A sudden shout made him jerk up his head, and he realized that he had been dozing. People all around him were pointing and shouting excitedly. He saw what they were pointing at: a group of men leading a bear cub. They had ropes tied around its neck, and each man held the end of one rope, controlling the movement of the cub, bringing it slowly into the clearing.

Matsuzo felt a tug on his arm and saw that Mopi was sitting next to him. She was grinning and her eyes were bright with excitement. "Our bear," she whispered to him.

Matsuzo recognized the bear cub as the one in the cage by the entrance of the headman's house. It had reminded him of his puppy, Taro. Mopi had been giving the bear cub treats for months, she said, and she was proud to see her pet taking the leading role in the ceremony, whatever it was.

The headman stood up, and in his hands was a short bow. As he notched the arrow, a hush fell over the crowd, and even the bear cub stopped struggling. What was the headman going to shoot at? wondered Matsuzo. Perhaps he would aim the arrow into the air, like Zenta, and bring down a bird.

Then, as he stared with unbelieving eyes, Matsuzo saw the headman shoot straight at the bear cub. It roared with pain and began to struggle, but the ropes held it in place. Another arrow hit the cub in the breast. The archer was the hunter uncle. Other men shot: Tonkuru, Ashiri, the men who had been in the rescue party at the shipwreck. . . .

A wave of nausea rose choking in Matsuzo's chest. He seemed to see his puppy, Taro, writhing and bristling with arrows. Mopi! What was she feeling, to see her pet cruelly done to death like this? He whirled around to look at the girl beside him.

He found her staring at the slaughter with huge eyes and her mouth stretched wide. Was she going to scream? Her shoulders shook, and a shrill giggle burst from her. She was becoming hysterical.

Then she tugged at his arm again. "Good! Good!" she whispered fiercely. "Bear now happy!" Her eyes were shining with joy. Not sadness. Not hysteria at losing her pet. Joy.

Matsuzo tore his arm from her grasp and

jumped to his feet. He wanted to weep, to throw up, to escape from these savages. More than anything he wanted to get away from Mopi.

Before he could turn away, a hand clamped down on his shoulder. "Don't do anything!" whispered Zenta's voice. "Not if you want to stay alive."

Matsuzo slowly turned to look at his friend. Zenta's face was set like iron. "I don't enjoy this any more than you do," he said. "But we must not do anything to disturb this festival. It's the most important event of the year for the Ainu people, and it matters deeply to them."

Swallowing hard to control his nausea, Matsuzo nodded and sat down again. He stole a quick glance at Mopi. She was still entranced by the shooting, and had not noticed his movement.

Zenta sat down beside Matsuzo and leaned over. "Remember: The bear is probably numb and doesn't feel much, since those arrows are poisoned with aconite."

Matsuzo wasn't sure whether Zenta meant his words as a comfort or as a warning. He closed his eyes and tried to think of something else—but all he could think of was Mopi offering treats and cooing words of endearment to her pet. He tried to shut his ears to the thuds of the arrows and the grunts of the dying animal. To his immense relief, the noise stopped after a while, and then a general cheering sounded from the crowd.

He opened his eyes for a peek and quickly shut them tight again. Several hunters, led by Tonkuru's uncle, were skinning the dead animal with sharp knives. The smell of fresh blood made Matsuzo's stomach heave again, and he concentrated all his attention on breathing evenly.

Matsuzo wasn't sure how much time had passed. He was aware that a deep silence had fallen over the crowd. Then he felt Zenta's hand on his arm. "You can look now," said his friend. "It's over."

A bizarre sight met his eyes. In the middle of the clearing the bear cub lay flat on its stomach, with its head pointing toward the headman's house. It lay very flat, and then Matsuzo realized that it was just the skin of the bear, with legs, claws, and head still attached. The rest of the carcass had been dragged away.

The headman approached the bearskin and placed an offering in front of the slack jaws. The offering was some fruit on a Japanese lacquered dish. The use of the lacquered dish—a utensil from a civilized world—struck Matsuzo as particularly macabre. Other men placed their offerings of foods and decorated objects, such as carved wooden vessels, beads, and medallions.

Matsuzo felt a tug from Mopi again. "Soon we feast. Eat bear meat!"

The young samurai could no longer control himself. He jumped up, rushed to the edge of the clearing, and vomited behind some trees.

Zenta followed Matsuzo to the trees. His own stomach was feeling queasy by the time the younger man had finished retching. The two of them sat shivering in silence, trying to ignore the gruesome sounds coming from the center of the crowd. After the headman's bear cub had been killed and skinned, the cubs from the other households had been dragged to the clearing and were undergoing the same fate.

Huddled by the trees, away from the fires and the people, Zenta found it bitterly cold. Not a great drinker of wine, he nevertheless felt that this was one time when he would welcome a flask of warm sake—several flasks.

It was nearly dark when the festival ended, and the various families of the kotan went their own way, carrying the bloody pieces of bear meat that were their share. Mopi glanced at Matsuzo and started to approach him, but was led away by her mother.

The two samurai silently followed Ashiri and his wife home. Zenta hoped that none of the celebrants at the festival had noticed their desertion from the circle.

But it had not escaped Tonkuru's sharp eyes. Very few things did. He accompanied them to Ashiri's house, and at the door he drew Zenta aside for some private conversation.

"Your friend was not feeling well?" he asked.

"He's not used to the food," said Zenta. "I know that you've all done your best to provide for us, but we are simply accustomed to a different diet."

He didn't think that Tonkuru really believed his answer, but it saved face—on both sides.

"Mopi is disappointed that your friend left so suddenly," remarked Tonkuru. "He was horrified by the sacrifices, wasn't he?"

It was pointless to pretend. "Yes, I'm afraid he was," replied Zenta. "We Japanese are Buddhists, you see, and it is against our religion to kill living things."

"And yet you kill *people*," said Tonkuru. He seemed genuinely puzzled by the inconsistency. "You and your friend belong to the samurai class, and your profession is to kill people."

"No, that's not true!" said Zenta. He felt defensive. The samurai, with their ready swords, *had* been called hired killers often enough. But Zenta really wanted this young Ainu to have a different

69

opinion of him. "Our true profession is to serve our feudal lord," he said carefully. "We kill only when it is necessary." It was a weak answer, and he knew it.

Tonkuru was silent for a moment. "We don't think of our bear ritual as a killing," he said finally. He spoke earnestly, and seemed just as anxious as Zenta to make his listener understand. "Rather, it is our way of honoring the Bear Spirit, who comes to the feast as our guest. You see, the Bear Spirit provides us with invaluable meat, fat, and skins. We don't consider the bear as prey to be hunted down. It comes to the Ainu people and generously offers itself to us. At the festival we are thanking the Bear Spirit and showing him that we accept his offering."

"I see . . . so the bear is your guest of honor," said Zenta. And, in a way, he *did* see. He smiled wryly. "We are your guests, too. I just hope you don't honor us the same way."

Tonkuru laughed. Then he beat his arms against his chest. "Why are we standing outside here, in the cold? Let's go inside and talk more comfortably."

Inside the house, Zenta found Matsuzo already stretched out on his sleeping mat by the fire pit. He was sound asleep, probably exhausted by emotion. Okera had hung some reed mats in front of her corner, giving her a rough sort of privacy. Ashiri himself was sitting in the opposite corner, tightening the cords around the head of one of his spears. He looked up unsmiling at the entrance of his younger brother and Zenta, muttered a brief word, and went back to his task.

Tonkuru sat down and held his hands out toward the warmth from the embers of the fire. Zenta sat down beside him. "Have your people decided that we're free to go to the Japanese settlement?" he asked.

Tonkuru sighed. "I'm afraid the answer is no— at least for the present."

Zenta was keenly disappointed. He had been hoping that both Tonkuru and his father would be well disposed toward them. "Do you agree with the decision?"

"I personally believe that it will serve our interests better to let you go," replied Tonkuru. "Then you can tell your countrymen about us, about our desire to be on good terms with them."

"That we will most certainly do," Zenta said quickly. "Did the others think that we would go and spread slander about your people?"

Again Tonkuru sighed. "That's not the reason why they don't want to let you go. You see, the men who have met you suspect that you are a strong and dangerous warrior. If you add your strength to that of the settlers, things will go hard with us in case of a conflict."

"Why do you think there will be a conflict?" demanded Zenta. "Why can't you and the settlers live in peace?"

"*I* believe that we can live in peace, whatever the other men in the kotan think," said Tonkuru. His voice was bitter. "But the choice may not be ours. Your countrymen may attack first, and already they complain about provocations on our part."

"And have there been any?" asked Zenta.

There was a sharp comment from Ashiri, and an equally sharp answer from Tonkuru. Zenta guessed that the elder brother did understand a little Japanese after all. He and Matsuzo would have to be more careful how they spoke in Ashiri's presence.

Tonkuru turned to Zenta again. "My brother says the settlers are lying, and that we have done nothing to provoke them."

Zenta noticed that Tonkuru did not say whether he himself thought there had been provocations. But before he could ask more questions, the young Ainu rose to his feet, stretched, and yawned. "It's late, and I should go home."

Although Tonkuru did not have the heavy build and muscular strength of his elder brother, he looked alert and intelligent. He will make a good headman, thought Zenta.

Having walked with Tonkuru to the entrance, Zenta stopped. "You can't keep us here indefinitely, you know."

The young Ainu did not miss the threat in Zenta's words. "Please don't do anything rash," he said. "Nothing good will come of it, either for you or for us. I'll try to talk to the others again."

But in the meantime the others might take action on their own, thought Zenta. If they believed that he was a danger to them, they might never let him or Matsuzo leave the Ainu settlement alive. Tonkuru was powerless to prevent one of the other men from trying to kill the two of them. Accidents could be arranged: a careless tripping of a cord attached to a poisoned spring bow, for example, or a fall into an icy stream, with no one nearby to prevent them from dying of exposure.

They had to find some way to escape, decided Zenta. He was also worried about Matsuzo's leg, for the redness and swelling did not seem to be improving very fast. Although his young friend tried not to show anything, it was obvious that his leg was giving him pain. Zenta was afraid that the black Ainu ointment might be doing Matsuzo's wound more harm than good.

In a way, Zenta regretted that he must leave the Ainus, for they were a brave and generous people. Besides, as Tonkuru said, he could really help in preventing a conflict if he could reach the Japanese settlement and report that the Ainus wanted to live in peace with them.

Zenta knew that for Matsuzo, every hour spent among the Ainus was misery. His leg required treatment by a competent physician. But aside from that, his friend found it hard to adjust to the Ainu way of life. He had left home a little more than a year ago, when his family had lost their employment with a warlord defeated in the civil wars. Up to that time, Matsuzo had known only the comforts of a home with high standards of cleanliness and decorum.

Zenta himself, however, had left home at the age of fifteen, and during his ten years of wandering he had experienced extremes of hunger and squalor. He didn't enjoy eating Ainu food, but it was better than starving. He didn't enjoy the miasma of unwashed bodies, but it was better than that of rotting corpses after a battle.

There was still so much to see and learn by staying with the Ainus. He was beginning to feel a rapport even with the moody Ashiri. In time he might master a little of the Ainu language, and then he could talk to them about hunting, about traps, and about plants and animals he had not seen on the Japanese mainland.

Unfortunately, there seemed to be a growing hostility between the Ainus and the Japanese, and it would be dangerous for the two of them to stay. But how could they hope to escape? They would not be able to go fast because of Matsuzo's leg. How could they make their way through the woods, filled with hidden traps? They would leave telltale prints in the snow, or they would starve or die of exposure before finding the settlement.

They needed help. And help came from a totally unexpected source.

FIVE

Before they could begin to think of escaping, said Zenta, they had to distance themselves from Ashiri. Their reluctant host had been assigned the thankless task of keeping them always in sight, so wherever they went, he was at their elbow.

"Ashiri doesn't enjoy being our nursemaid," said Zenta. "It won't take much to get him so thoroughly exasperated with us that he'll hate the sight of us."

The two Japanese began their campaign of exasperation by insisting on going fishing. They knew that Ashiri didn't want to go fishing. It was the morning after the Bear Festival, and with all the fresh meat he had brought back with him, he would feel little need to go into the icy water and spear fish.

The two Japanese pretended not to see Ashiri's reluctance. Pointing to the gobs of dark bear meat hanging on the drying poles, Matsuzo made a face and produced a gagging sound, which his mother would have called extremely ill bred. But it was quite successful in indicating to Ashiri his disgust at the sight of fresh meat.

Zenta joined the charade by pointing to some pieces of dried salmon and grinning idiotically, to indicate an uncontrollable Japanese craving for fish. Then the two of them turned and started for the stream where Ashiri had fished earlier. If you don't feel like fishing, you don't have to go with us, their action said plainly.

Just as plainly, Ashiri growled a command for them to stay put. Then he rushed into the house, and quickly returned with a couple of his fishing spears. He was following his orders not to let them roam around the area unattended.

"Well, that didn't work," Matsuzo said to Zenta out of the corner of his mouth.

"I didn't expect it would," said Zenta. "But if we keep this up, we'll wear him out sooner or later."

Matsuzo brightened. "That's true! He has his chores and his duties, and we're wasting his valuable time."

Ashiri frowned darkly at the two Japanese, clearly suspecting that they were plotting something. But there was no way to stop them from talking to each other.

At the stream the Ainu peered carefully around at the trees on the opposite bank, where he had seen the lurking Japanese earlier. Satisfied that there was no one hiding there, Ashiri handed one of the spears to Zenta, and the two men waded into the stream. Today, the ice at the edges seemed thinner. Spring was around the corner, even in this northern country.

On the bank Matsuzo watched the two men. Both had a quality of stillness that he envied. The only movement came from the curly hairs at the edges of their furred cloaks, stirred a little by the breeze. Someday, Matsuzo thought, he might achieve this degree of stillness, if he worked at it.

Suddenly, Ashiri's spear stabbed into the water, and it came out with a wriggling fish, a big one. A murmur of admiration came from Zenta. As before, some of Ashiri's sullenness lifted and he came close to smiling.

Zenta's spear splashed into the water, but it came up empty. He grinned ruefully, and both men went back to staring at the stream.

Matsuzo shivered. He stood up and swung his arms about, looking around for some activity that could keep him warm. A clump of birch trees stood close to him, and he ran his hands down their smooth trunks, admiring their stark whiteness. They were unlike any of the trees he had seen at home. He noticed idly that one of the tree trunks was marred by some scratches. Then he peered harder at the tree trunk, and his heart began to thump. There was no mistake: What he was looking at was writing—writing in the Japanese phonetic script.

To an Ainu, whose culture did not include writing, these were meaningless scratches—made by the claws of a squirrel or a bird, perhaps. To Matsuzo, they said, "Under the big rock to the left of the trees."

There was indeed a big, flat rock a short step away from the base of the birch trees. Matsuzo stole a quick glance at the two men in the stream. They were still concentrating on the swimming fish. Then, bending down with his back to the stream, he carefully lifted the rock. Underneath was a small, flat packet wrapped in oiled paper. He tore open the covering and saw a piece of paper with a drawing on it: It was a map, and he could see the stream clearly marked on it, and some hills. But before he could examine the map more closely, he heard a shout from the stream. He quickly stuffed the packet into his sleeve and turned around.

Zenta was gleefully holding his spear aloft, with a fish impaled at the end of it. It was very small, but a fish it undoubtedly was. Even Ashiri was smiling broadly.

Zenta waded to the bank and climbed out. "I'd better stop now, before my toes freeze and drop off."

Matsuzo bent down and pretended to admire Zenta's catch. "We have to find a chance to talk privately," he whispered. "I've found something under that big rock over there. It might help us."

They finally had their chance that night when Ashiri and his wife had retired behind their reed screens. Not knowing when the Ainus might peek out at them made it difficult to speak freely, even though they didn't think Ashiri understood very much. There was still a faint light from the fire in the pit, since Okera was careful never to let the fire die out completely. The two Japanese lay on their stomachs and eagerly examined the map.

Four things hindered their escape from the Ainus. Matsuzo was unable to walk quickly. There were hidden traps that could be triggered by a careless step on the trails. They would leave foot-prints in the snow, which the Ainus, expert hunters and trappers, could easily follow. Finally, and this was the greatest obstacle, they did not know their way in this unknown country. Once lost, they would not survive long in the harsh, cold climate.

The map would help overcome this last difficulty. "Well? Shall we try for an escape?" Zenta asked, his voice the merest wisp of a breath.

Matsuzo nodded.

They put their plan to work the very next morning. They indicated a desire to accompany Okera in looking for fern tips. They had already learned from Mopi that hunting and fishing were activities for the menfolk, while gathering plants was the work of the womenfolk. But the two Japanese, pretending ignorance of the custom, happily followed Okera as she headed for the forest with her basket to look for the early tips of the bracken fern. After a winter diet of meat, fish, and roots, it was a tempting treat to have fresh greens. Zenta went so far as to carry Okera's basket for her.

Ashiri looked disgusted. Even if he had admired Zenta's skill with the bow and had been impressed by his rapid improvement with the fishing spear, he obviously thought that doing a woman's work was beneath the dignity of a man and a warrior.

His gloomy expression darker than usual, Ashiri doggedly accompanied his wife and his two guests. Okera, obviously enjoying her husband in the undignified role of a follower, constantly looked back and giggled.

It was clear to Matsuzo that well before the middle of the morning, Ashiri was thoroughly tired of the two Japanese, of fern shoots, and even of his wife. Okera simpered and her blue-rimmed mouth stretched to show white, even teeth.

The two Japanese rushed around cheerfully. They whooped and burrowed into the undergrowth for the new green tips. They didn't find a single fern, but they succeeded in thoroughly churning the ground.

"I have to give my leg a rest," muttered Matsuzo to Zenta. "Besides, my cheeks are getting a cramp from smiling so much."

"Let's separate," suggested Zenta. "You stay here, and I'll go in that direction."

His maneuver forced Ashiri to swivel his head this way and that, trying to keep both of them in sight. It was obvious that they were successful in wearing down their Ainu host. Matsuzo could now tell the difference between Ashiri's normal dour expression and his scowl of exasperation.

The Ainu's face was actually quite expressive, Matsuzo realized to his surprise.

"We didn't do badly," he said as they returned from their food-gathering expedition. "One more day of this, and he will not only let us go, but speed us on our way."

Zenta grinned. "After turning his head so much, he has his neck almost tied in knots. I think we should make our break tomorrow morning."

That afternoon Tonkuru paid them a visit, accompanied by Mopi. The little girl looked shy for the first time. On seeing her, Matsuzo could not quite hide his revulsion. He still had a vivid memory of her delight during the slaughter of the bear cub. Mopi must have sensed his reaction, for she didn't ask to see his wound this time. Her eyes grew enormous and she retreated until she was hidden by her brother.

Tonkuru glanced back at his sister. "She wants to know if she has offended you in some way," he told the young samurai.

"I'm . . . I'm sorry," Matsuzo apologized lamely. He felt a twinge of guilt, but could not quite conquer his distaste. "It's nothing that Mopi has done. It's just that I'm not used to animals being killed for meat. Seeing . . . seeing so many bear cubs slaughtered upset my stomach."

Tonkuru nodded gravely. Then he turned and

said a few words to Mopi. She answered in a low voice, stole a quick glance at Matsuzo, then retreated to the corner of the room where Ashiri's wife had set up her weaving loom. Okera pulled the little girl down and gave her some elm bark fibers to twist. Soon the two were busy at the loom.

"Ashiri told me that you've been fishing," Tonkuru said, smiling and turning to Zenta. "You've also been gathering ferns. So it's true that you'd do anything to avoid eating the bear meat."

Zenta smiled back. "We were also looking for some way to pass the time." His face became serious. "Have you made any progress in persuading the others to let us go?"

"No, because there's been a complication," Tonkuru said heavily. "It's been reported that someone in the Japanese settlement has been badly injured, and the people there are very angry. They accuse us of causing the injury."

"If you let us go to the settlement, we can help convince the people there that you are innocent," said Zenta. He looked at the young Ainu and added, "If you *are* innocent. What happened, do you know?"

"I'm not sure, exactly," replied Tonkuru.

He may not really be lying, thought Matsuzo, but he's pretty evasive.

That night the two samurai studied the map together one last time. "Will your leg be well enough tomorrow for walking the whole distance?" asked Zenta.

"It will have to be," Matsuzo replied soberly. "If we don't reach the settlement soon, my leg may not get well at all."

Their plan was to separate during the first part of their escape, but they had neither the time nor the means to make a copy of the map. Therefore Matsuzo was to keep the map with him, and Zenta would have to memorize one portion of it, and then agree on a place where they could meet once they were well away from the kotan.

"You can put it away now," Zenta said finally. "I think I can find my way to the second hill beyond the river. We should meet there."

Matsuzo nodded, then carefully folded the map and thrust it into his sleeve. He froze. There was a faint slithering sound at the entrance. Who could it be? Judging from the snores, he knew Ashiri was asleep behind the screens.

Zenta had heard the slithering sound as well. He put a warning hand for a moment on Matsuzo's arm, and then lay back on his mat. Matsuzo followed his example. He breathed deeply and regularly, but kept his eyes open a slit. His right hand gripped the hilt of his sword.

The reed mat at the entrance lifted and Okera walked into the room on silent feet. She glanced quickly at the two guests on their sleeping mats, seemed reassured, then turned and went behind the screens where her husband lay. Matsuzo heard some faint movements, a snore from Ashiri, and after that, nothing.

A wife who stole out at night. Matsuzo thought about Okera's laughter when they were gathering fern tips with her. She enjoyed the company of men, obviously. Was she tired of her husband? Ashiri was a strong, muscular man, a good provider, and an expert fisherman. Some wives could do much worse. But he did have a surly temperament, and perhaps Okera wanted livelier companionship. Perhaps she was just going to the outhouse—although her expression looked too furtive for that. Matsuzo decided that Ashiri's unfaithful wife—if she was unfaithful—was not his business. He and Zenta were planning to escape the next morning, and he needed rest.

Early in the morning all the men of the kotan were called out to work on repairing a deer fence in preparation for the spring hunting season. The fence was a wooden barrier built across a known deer run, and it slowed the herd so that the hunters would be able to get in some good shots before the animals jumped over. The fence was built to last several years, but it needed annual repairs to patch some of the inevitable breaks.

For Zenta and Matsuzo the work on the fence presented opportunities to move around without arousing suspicion. They went along with the work gang and made themselves very helpful by carrying pieces of wood where needed. Ashiri was no longer staying close to them. *He's tired of us and is probably expecting one or the other of his friends to keep us in sight,* Matsuzo thought.

Gradually, the two ronin separated. While Matsuzo went with one group of men to fetch more wood, Zenta stayed with the group weaving more sticks into the fence to strengthen it. Then, as planned, the two men changed places. Their purpose was to get the Ainus used to seeing one, but not both, of them at the same time.

By the middle of the morning, Matsuzo knew that the time had come. He was with the work crew at the fence, and their supply of sticks was low. He swallowed and, waving one of the few remaining sticks, said he needed to fetch more wood. His voice was a little unsteady, and in any case the Ainu working beside him didn't understand a word, but the gesture was clear enough.

Matsuzo rose, controlled the trembling in his

legs, and limped away. Despite himself, he stole a glance back at Ashiri. Their careful preparation had not been not wasted: Ashiri didn't even bother to look at him.

Just as he thought he was safely out of sight, he came face to face with one of the workmen, who was carrying a bundle of sticks. The Ainu asked him a question sharply. Matsuzo's mind became a complete blank. Without quite knowing what he was doing, he reached out and took over the bundle of sticks.

It turned out to be the best thing he could have done. The Ainu nodded as if satisfied and went back to gathering more sticks.

Despite the cold, Matsuzo's face was drenched with sweat. He pretended to take a few steps in the direction of the work gang at the fence. When he was sure the Ainu was out of sight, he dropped the bundle of sticks and let out his breath in a deep sigh. He waited until his heart had stopped pounding, and then he took out the map for a final look before starting out for the Japanese settlement.

In the beginning, the going was easy. His leg was giving him less trouble than he had expected. Perhaps Mopi was right: Movement actually helped the leg to heal.

Matsuzo knew that with all the work party trampling around gathering wood, footprints would be thoroughly crisscrossed and impossible to identify. It was also safe to assume that there would be no hidden traps nearby, since the men or children of the kotan could trigger them and get hurt.

But when he had gone some distance away from the Ainu kotan, the only footprints on the snow were his own. He began to walk more slowly, and peered anxiously at the ground, alert for the sight of a cord across the path—a cord attached to the trigger of a spring bow. Zenta had told him that the traps were meant for deer and other game, not for men. Therefore the Ainus might not make a point of hiding the cord from human eyes. But perhaps Zenta was just trying to be comforting.

According to the map, Matsuzo knew that he was nearly one third of the way to the Japanese settlement. Soon he would reach the place where he and Zenta had agreed to meet. Perhaps Ashiri and the other workers had already noticed their absence and started the pursuit. Once they were on the right track, the Ainus would soon overtake them.

But it might be some time before they got on the right track—or rather right tracks, for the essential part of Zenta's plan was that the two of them go separately. By the time their pursuers had sorted out all the footprints and discovered which were those of the two fugitives, they would find that the two pairs of prints went in different directions.

Matsuzo proceeded very cautiously, alert for every flicker and rustle. His senses were keen, for his training as a samurai made him aware of anything threatening or out of place—in his own country. The problem was, he did not know what was normal and what was out of place here on this northern island of Ezo. In this primeval forest neither he nor Zenta was a match for the native Ainus.

There! He heard a crackling of the underbrush. Could it be Zenta? He was very close to their appointed rendezvous. The noise grew louder, and his heart began to beat faster. Whoever made that noise was not trying to be stealthy. Zenta would have approached cautiously. It must be one of their Ainu pursuers.

His hand tightened on the hilt of his sword. Then he realized that he wasn't sure if he could bring himself to draw his sword on his pursuer—on an Ainu, who had saved him from drowning and exposure, who had housed him and fed him.

A violent rustle this time, and much closer. It

made him wonder. All the Ainus he had seen so far moved gracefully and economically, making very little noise. Who could it be?

Then a figure emerged from behind the thick trunk of a pine tree. What he saw made the breath catch in his throat: It was the huge, shaggy figure of a brown bear.

For a full minute the bear and the man stood motionless, staring at each other. Then the bear turned its head slightly. It seemed to be sniffing. Matsuzo knew very little about bears, but he had heard that they had very sensitive noses. He also knew that they were supposed to pass the winter asleep in a deep cave. This was still winter.

To Matsuzo's immense relief, the bear turned away and lumbered off. He listened to its crackling passage until it became a faint rustle in the distance. Then, feeling dizzy, he sank down on a log. He had forgotten to breathe.

Gradually, his heart became quiet again, and he was just about to raise his head when he felt a touch on his shoulder. "Are you all right?" asked a soft voice.

Matsuzo gasped and gave a violent start, but he sank back down when he saw that it was Zenta. "You frightened me! Why didn't you warn me you were coming?"

Zenta looked at him curiously. "I didn't want to

announce my arrival to the whole world, but I did clear my throat. You were too preoccupied to notice."

Matsuzo wiped his brow with his sleeve. "I was trying to recover from my meeting with a bear."

Zenta became still. "Are you sure it was a bear?" he asked. "They are supposed to hibernate during the winter."

"You think I saw an exceptionally hairy Ainu, perhaps?" growled Matsuzo. "It was a bear, I'm positive. I've seen quite a few captive bears recently, and I know what they look like."

"Very puzzling," Zenta said finally. "But we don't have time to worry about your encounter. We'd better move on, before our pursuers catch up with us."

"We're more than halfway to the settlement," said Matsuzo. He began to feel optimistic. "If we reach the river safely, our problems are over. According to the map, that's the place to cross, so it must be shallow enough to ford."

They reached the river safely, but their problems were not over. One of their Ainu pursuers had anticipated them, and was standing by the edge of the river, waiting. They had a choice of openly confronting the man, or doubling back and trying to find another crossing much farther up the river.

The Ainu's keen ears had heard their approach. He turned to face them, and Matsuzo saw that it was Tonkuru. "Don't be afraid," said the young Ainu. "I came alone, and none of the others know that you are here."

Before Matsuzo could stop him, Zenta walked out of the cover of the trees and approached Tonkuru. "So you guessed that we would come this way."

Tonkuru smiled. "The work party at the deer fence expected to catch up with you almost immediately. They didn't think that two strangers, wandering around in an unknown country, would get very far. But when they failed to find you, I suspected that you were headed for the Japanese settlement. And this is the best place to ford the river."

What were they going to do with this young man? Again, Matsuzo felt a strong reluctance to attack him.

"But I'm curious," continued Tonkuru. "How did you find your way here? Someone must have helped you. Who was it?"

"Perhaps we were following in the steps of the bear," said Zenta. He was watching the young Ainu very closely.

Tonkuru frowned. Although he was not tall, nor muscular like his brother, he looked like a bad enemy to cross. "What bear?" he asked quietly. "I don't understand."

Zenta smiled. "I don't understand, either. It was quite puzzling." His face became serious. "We're going to cross the river here and join the Japanese settlement. You and your people have saved our lives and shown us nothing but kindness, and I should like to part as friends. Please don't try to stop us."

"I don't have any intention of trying to stop you," said Tonkuru. "Almost from the first, I've tried to persuade the others to let you go."

He sounded sincere, and Matsuzo felt a rush of sympathy for him. "Thank you for everything you've done to help us." With difficulty, he added, "Please tell Mopi that I'm grateful to her for tending my leg, and I'm sorry I was brusque with her. Perhaps I'll see her again someday, and we'll be friends once more."

"We'll never forget our debt to your people," Zenta told Tonkuru. "One of the reasons we're so eager to reach the Japanese settlement is to tell them about your kindness to us. Perhaps that will convince them to keep the peace."

Tonkuru nodded gravely. "Yes, that is what I was hoping you'd undertake to do." He hesitated for a moment. "There is a message that I'd like you to give someone at the settlement."

"Of course," said Zenta promptly. "Who is it?"

Tonkuru did not reply immediately. Finally he sighed. "I'd like you to find a woman called Setona, and tell her that . . . that . . . I have not given up hope." He turned abruptly, and disappeared into the forest.

Well before dark the two men saw the fence surrounding the Japanese settlement. Soon they were close enough to make out some of the roofs rising above the fence. At the sight of the familiar-looking roofs, Matsuzo felt tears starting. He had to clear his throat before he could speak. "They'll probably take us for Ainus, with our beards and our dirty, smelly clothes."

He was right. Before they could get any closer, they heard shouts and alarms being given. Soon a detachment of armed men ran forward with swords unsheathed.

"We're Japanese!" shouted Zenta. "We've been staying with the Ainus, but we managed to escape."

There were some mutters, and then one of the armed men stepped forward. "So you're the ones I saw the other day. You found my map, then."

SIX

Matsuzo did not want to get out of the bath. It was pure bliss to sit soaking in the fragrant cedar tub. After the first shock of entering the hot water, his leg had stopped hurting. That was the best thing of all: discovering that his leg was well on its way to healing.

They had found a physician in the settlement, and when the man had peeled off the ragged bandage, he had nodded his approval. "That's good. This is an Ainu ointment, you say? It did an excellent job of combating the poisons you got from the scrape."

Matsuzo didn't believe him at first. "You mean

this black stuff actually helped me?"

The physician smiled. "The natives know more than we realize about the medicinal powers of the local plants. You must have been treated by an experienced medicine man."

Matsuzo didn't tell him that the "experienced medicine man" was a little girl. He asked if it was safe to get his leg wet, for he could not wait to step into a bathtub.

"Of course," replied the physician. "Soaking will do it good."

Once in the tub, Matsuzo found that he didn't have the energy to climb out again. He was almost asleep when he heard Zenta's voice.

"You can't wallow there all night," said Zenta. "The local commander wants to see both of us."

Zenta had already shaved, and his hair had been oiled and tied neatly into a topknot. He was dressed in a kimono of steel gray, and he held out a folded kimono of the same color. It was a color Matsuzo had not seen in the costumes of the Ainu people. He climbed out of the tub, welcoming the thought of putting on decent clothes at last.

Matsuzo dressed and shaved off his beard, not an easy task since it had been growing for more than two weeks. It was also a pleasure to oil his hair and tie it up again into a neat topknot. He hoped that the aromatic hair oil would mask any lingering smells on him of fish, bear, and deer fat.

Looking at the pile of Ainu clothing lying on the ground, he kicked at them disgustedly. "I can hardly wait to burn these clothes."

"No!" said Zenta. "I want to keep them. They're mementos of our adventures. Besides, some of the settlers might want to examine these garments."

"But they reek!" cried Matsuzo. "No amount of washing will get them completely clean, especially that fur cape!"

"Strange—I didn't notice the smell when I was actually wearing the clothes," remarked Zenta.

"*You* may not have noticed the smell, but I assure you that everyone else in the settlement did." The speaker had approached the bathhouse, and was regarding the two ronin with a wide grin.

Matsuzo recognized him as the man who had greeted them when they had first arrived. He was the one who had left the map for them under the rock. They had learned that his name was Jimbei.

"We haven't had a chance to thank you properly for leaving us the map," said Zenta. "Without it we would never have found the settlement."

The man called Jimbei smiled even more widely. He was not very tall, but stocky and strongly made. When he smiled, two bracketlike dimples appeared on either side of his mouth, making him look so droll that Matsuzo found himself grinning in response.

"I saw you fishing in the stream and thought you were Ainu at first," said Jimbei. "But when I heard you speak, I knew you were Japanese. I didn't know whether you were living with the Ainus because you chose to, so I left you the map just in case you wanted to escape."

"And a good thing you did!" Matsuzo said gratefully. "We certainly didn't stay with the Ainus out of choice. We were shipwrecked on the coast here, and they saved us from drowning."

"They did more than save us from drowning," Zenta reminded Matsuzo. "They fed us and gave us clothes to keep us warm."

Jimbei looked curiously at Zenta. When he wasn't smiling, his eyes were searching and shrewd. "Our commander will be glad to hear all about your experiences among the Ainus. In fact you can be quite helpful to us here."

They left the communal bathhouse, which was one of the larger buildings in the settlement. Jimbei led them down a narrow, muddy road, lined on both sides with small wooden houses. Some of them still had the resinous smell of new pine wood. The roofs were planks held down with rocks, and the buildings seemed constructed with more haste than taste. They might be little more than shacks, but after spending more than a week in outlandish Ainu houses, Matsuzo beamed affectionately at them.

"Your commander here has a sizeable military force?" Zenta asked.

Jimbei's eyes looked over the two ronin unhurriedly before he answered. "We have just a small portion of the Japanese forces on Ezo, since our settlement is modest compared to other centers. Commander Kato here is connected to the Matsumae family, who were the first to settle people systematically in Ezo."

"The Matsumaes are an offshoot of the Takeda family, aren't they?" asked Zenta.

"Oho, so you know that already?" said Jimbei. Again, he studied Zenta. His eyes widened a little. "Where did you say you're from?"

"I didn't say," replied Zenta.

Jimbei waited, and when Zenta did not elaborate, he smiled. "Well, we're a miscellaneous group here, but we're not all vagabonds and outcasts."

Arriving at a substantial building surrounded by a fence, Jimbei asked the two ronin to wait at the gate while he went inside to announce them.

"Maybe he lists us among the outcasts and the vagabonds," muttered Matsuzo. "I suppose he thinks we're here to beg for a bowl of rice and a futon to sleep on."

"But that's exactly what we *are* begging for," said Zenta.

Before Matsuzo could muster a retort, Jimbei returned. "Commander Kato will see you now."

Commander Kato, seated on a cushion in his reception hall, had a huge pointed head, almost no neck, and very short arms. With his legs tucked under him, he looked like one of those pear-shaped *daruma* dolls, which immediately swung back up again every time they were pushed down.

Coming out of a big round belly, his voice was surprisingly breathless. "So you are the two men who managed to survive, after spending more than a week with the natives!" He started to wheeze, and it took Matsuzo a moment to realize that the commander was laughing.

"Without the Ainus, we certainly wouldn't have survived," Zenta said quietly. "We were nearly dying of thirst and hunger when they rescued us from the sea."

"Hee, hee, hee," wheezed Commander Kato, rocking back and forth with laughter but always regaining his upright position. "They fed you raw bear meat, didn't they? How did it taste?"

"We're wasting time," said the deep voice of the

man sitting to one side of the commander. He had a thin, leathery face, and a deep line between his eyes, so he seemed to be frowning darkly. Matsuzo was to learn that even when the man smiled, the deep line between his eyes remained.

"My steward—hee, hee—thinks I'm too frivolous," said Commander Kato. "Let's see, now . . ." He looked helplessly at the steward. "What was I supposed to ask them?"

The steward glanced at Zenta. "We need information about the Ainu camp and about their methods of defense. Jimbei is the only man who has gotten close to them, but he has never entered one of their homes."

"Does that mean you regard the Ainus as enemies, my lord?" asked Zenta. "Do you have a reason for doing so?"

Commander Kato blinked at Zenta's question. He turned again to his steward. "Why do we regard the Ainus as enemies?"

The steward sighed. "The bear, my lord. Tell them about the bear."

"If you ask me," sniffed the commander, "I think someone is playing a joke on us and made up the story about the bear."

"Several people in the settlement, including a young boy, have been badly mauled, my lord," the steward said patiently. "If it's a joke, it's a joke in very bad taste."

Commander Kato pouted. "Since you know so much, why don't *you* tell them about the bear?"

Matsuzo, itching with impatience to hear about the bear, was beginning to see why the steward was treating his master as a petulant child.

"If I may be allowed to speak," said a voice by the door. It was Jimbei, and this time there was no drollery in his face.

"Yes, of course, Jimbei," said Commander Kato, obviously relieved to have someone else speak up. "Tell us what you know."

Jimbei advanced into the room. "I was one of the first to see the bear . . ." he began.

"Did anyone else see it?" Commander Kato asked quickly.

"Several other people saw it," said Jimbei.

The commander sighed. "All right. Go on."

"It was early evening, and I was walking along the road leading to the gate," began Jimbei. He shivered a little. "I heard running steps; then there was a cry, sort of a gurgle."

"A gurgle?" asked the steward, his frown deepening. Perhaps he suspected Jimbei of facetiousness.

"The man who made it had his throat torn, so

that was the only sound he could make." Jimbei swallowed. "He still can't talk very well, even now."

"Yes, but what about the bear?" Commander Kato demanded.

"The injured man was lying on the ground, and standing over him was a monstrous bear. I was afraid he would attack me next. He didn't notice me, maybe because I was upwind from him. Other people came out of their doors and started yelling, and the bear ran off."

After Jimbei finished, there was a long, thoughtful silence. Commander Kato, rocking back and forth, broke the silence. "Aren't bears supposed to hibernate in the winter?"

Matsuzo cleared his throat. "I saw a bear as well, when we were on our way here from the Ainu camp."

"Ahh," said the steward. With the line deep between his eyes, he was still frowning, but Matsuzo's remark had obviously pleased him. "So! We have one more person who saw a bear."

Commander Kato was pouting again. "Get to the point," he told the steward.

"The bear was forced to awaken from his winter sleep by the Ainus, of course, who are skilled at controlling them. And they are training the bear to attack our people!"

"I don't see why the Ainus would want to do that," said the commander.

"Because they want to drive us away!" shouted the steward. Then he must have realized that he was showing disrespect to his superior. Moderating his voice, he continued, "They want to claim the whole of Ezo as theirs."

He turned his frowning gaze on Zenta. "What can you tell us about their warrior class?"

"I haven't noticed an exclusive warrior class," Zenta said slowly. "We met the headman and his sons, and they seem to live the same sort of life as the rest of the people. They hunt, they fish, and their womenfolk gather edible plants."

"Yes, but who does the fighting?" demanded the steward. "The headman and his sons?"

Zenta took a moment to think. "I haven't seen the headman using a weapon, although one of his sons is very skilled with his spear. Some of the hunters I met were expert bowmen." He added wryly, "But the spear was used for fish, and the bow for deer. Unlike our samurai, the Ainu rulers actually produce the food they eat."

"Hee, hee, hee," wheezed Commander Kato. "You have a sharp tongue. I like that."

The steward's frown was like a slash of black ink between his eyes. "But what about their weapons? Are they superior to ours?"

Before Zenta could answer, Matsuzo said, "The arrows! They have poisoned arrows!"

"I saw the Ainu man spearing a fish swimming in the water," said Jimbei. "I wouldn't want to face that spear in battle."

"You see?" the commander said to the steward. "These Ainus are formidable. We should think twice before getting into a fight with them."

"We don't have a choice!" cried the steward, his voice rising again. He took a deep breath and spoke more calmly. "But I'm sure our brave men can overcome these savages."

"I should mention the Ainus' most powerful weapon," said Zenta. "It's their knowledge of the country."

"He's got a point there!" wheezed Commander Kato. "The Ainus are not going to be obliging enough to fight us in a pitched battle. They're going to lead us over hill and dale, and around and around in circles."

To this last remark the steward was unable to think of a reply. Telling Jimbei to find suitable quarters for the two ronin, he dismissed them curtly.

Just before they left the room, Matsuzo saw something he had not noticed before. A sliding door in the back of the room, leading to an inner chamber, was slightly open. Through the crack he caught sight of someone peering intently at him. The eyes met his, and the person quickly withdrew. What struck him was that the eyes were the deep-set, round eyes of an Ainu. What was an Ainu doing in Commander Kato's house?

Outside the commander's gate, Jimbei looked more cheerful, and his dimples reappeared. "The steward has been looking for an excuse to fight. He used to be a notable warrior, you know, and life in this backwoods country doesn't agree with him." He looked slyly at the two ronin. "You don't seem like farmers, either. Perhaps you're escaping from someone on the mainland?"

That was a little too close for comfort. Jimbei had asked the question lightly, but he seemed genuinely eager to know the answer. Zenta answered him carefully. "We were caught up in some of the civil wars on the mainland. That's why we're not enthusiastic about getting into a fight here when there's no reason for it."

"I'm not enthusiastic either," Jimbei admitted cheerfully. "But these bear attacks—they're a good reason to fight. People's feelings here are running high."

Zenta moved his head slightly and flashed a glance back. It was done so quickly that Matsuzo would have missed it if he had not had a desire himself to look back. He sensed that they were being followed, followed very discreetly.

"How many people have been attacked?" Zenta asked Jimbei.

"Four, so far, including a little boy. He's only six years old."

"And they all said the attacker was a bear?"

Jimbei hesitated. Then he rolled his eyes comically and grinned. "All but the little boy. He thought it was a big man in a fur coat. He hadn't seen a bear before, so he wouldn't know what it was supposed to look like."

He stopped at a long, wooden building, more like a barracks than a private residence. "Sorry, this is the best I can do for you," he said. In spite of his words, he didn't look particularly apologetic. "There aren't too many women in the settlement yet. The Matsumaes tried to encourage permanent settlers in Ezo, but so far most of the people here are single men. Even the married ones have decided not to bring their families until they feel more secure about the safety here."

"From the way things look, they're not going to feel very secure," murmured Matsuzo.

Jimbei nodded, and his lips turned down. "The little boy who got mauled was the first child to be brought here. We won't be getting another child for a while."

He pushed open a sliding door of unpainted

wood. It was so new that the door did not slide quite smoothly in its groove. "I've brought the newcomers," he announced.

"They can have the corner room at the end," shouted a voice. "There are plenty of futons in the cupboard. Supper's at dusk, and latecomers eat what's left."

The figure accompanying the voice appeared briefly at the door, jerked his head at the two newcomers in a perfunctory bow, and went away as quickly as he had come.

The informality left Matsuzo slightly breathless. Even at the most humble farmhouses he had visited on the mainland, the farmer's wife would come forth and bow her head to the ground and make him welcome. The hospitality might be meager, but the willingness to serve was there.

Jimbei grinned. "We don't hold with much ceremony in a frontier settlement like this," he told the young ronin. "You'll get used to it. I frankly prefer it to all the bowing and scraping I used to go through."

He led them to the room at the end of the corridor. After what he had seen so far, Matsuzo was prepared for the bareness of the room. But at least the wooden floor was clean, and the room did not smell of fish oil and unwashed bodies. The large, sliding windows, covered with white paper, admitted a pleasant filtered light.

With a sigh of contentment, Matsuzo put down his long sword and sat cross-legged on the floor. It was almost like coming home again.

"I'll be back tomorrow morning," said Jimbei. "Then we can discuss what sort of work you want to do. There's not much agricultural work at this time of the year, but some of the men are digging a dry moat around the settlement. Maybe you can join one of the crews." He left after flashing his dimples at them one last time.

Matsuzo found his voice. "Well! What does he think we are? Farmers? Laborers?"

Zenta was peering out the window, and replied absently, "During the past week, we've speared fish and gathered fern tips. Why draw the line at being farmers and laborers?"

Matsuzo winced at Zenta's remark but had to admit it was true. "Well, I daresay I can put my back into digging a moat. It will be a change from building a deer fence, anyway."

He looked up at Zenta. "Someone followed us all the way from the commander's house, didn't he? Is he outside now?"

"I think he's coming in," murmured Zenta.

He was right. They heard the front door slide open unevenly in its groove, and then steps approaching along the hall. A voice asked hesitantly, "May I come in? I have a message from my mistress."

When Zenta grunted an assent, the door to the room slid open just enough to admit the head of a shy-looking young man. Or perhaps he was not shy, but merely unused to being a messenger. Matsuzo was beginning to discover that in a frontier settlement like this one, people had to take on jobs or positions they had not anticipated.

"My mistress is Setona," explained the young man, "who is of the household of the commander. She wants the opportunity to ask you some questions, and she would like to know if you could visit her this evening, after dusk."

Setona—the name was not Japanese, and Matsuzo guessed that it was Ainu. He suddenly remembered the deep-set, round eyes peering at them from the back of Commander Kato's reception room. They were Ainu eyes.

Moreover, he had heard the name Setona before. It was the name Tonkuru had mentioned just before he turned and disappeared back into the forest. Matsuzo could still picture the young Ainu's face: It had contained a mixture of wistfulness and sadness. But he had asked them to find Setona and tell her that he had not given up hope.

"Very well," Zenta told the messenger. "We'll

come to your mistress. Tell us where we should go."

The messenger gave the directions to a small house that was inside the gate to the commander's residence but separated from the main house.

After the messenger left, the two ronin looked at each other. "My guess is that Commander Kato has an Ainu mistress, this Setona," said Matsuzo. "That's why he isn't anxious to get into a war with them."

"If that's the case, then I'm very sorry for Tonkuru," said Zenta.

"Wait, you may be jumping to conclusions," Matsuzo pointed out. "Tonkuru may not be in love with Setona. Perhaps she's his sister, and he's hoping to rescue her from the Japanese."

"*You* are the one who is jumping to conclusions," retorted Zenta. "Setona need not be the commander's mistress at all. She might even be an old crone. Why don't we wait until we see her tonight before deciding?"

SEVEN

A person's social standing, Zenta knew, was revealed by certain clues: clothes, the style or location of residence, or how others behaved toward him. But with respect to Setona, the usual clues seemed to provide contradictory answers.

She did not live with the commander's family but in a separate pavilion and with her own serving people. That indicated a degree of independence. Therefore she was not a slave or a captive.

When the two ronin asked to be conducted to Setona's house, the guards and serving people they met showed respect, even fear, on hearing her name. But Zenta thought he also detected a touch of contempt in their attitude toward her.

As for clothes, Setona was dressed in a sober kimono suitable for a woman in a samurai family. Except for her unusual eyes and white skin, she looked quite Japanese. She was fine boned and had narrow hands and feet, unlike the Ainu women Zenta had seen, who seemed to have a heavier build. He guessed that she was of mixed blood.

Her manners were assured, and she spoke Japanese quite fluently as she greeted the two ronin. But there was something strange about her speech. Zenta finally realized what it was: She talked like a man, using words that sounded faintly comical when spoken in her feminine voice. She must have learned Japanese from her father, then. That meant her mixed blood had come from a Japanese father and an Ainu mother.

"I was eager to meet someone who was staying with my relatives," she said after the formalities were over.

Zenta looked at her curiously. "Are you related to the headman?"

"My mother was the headman's sister," Setona explained. "I've never been to her old home, but I've met my cousin Tonkuru and Ashiri's wife, Okera, when they came to the settlement to trade."

"Then there is still friendly contact between the Japanese and the Ainu people?" asked Zenta.

"There used to be," said Setona. "But recently things have become . . . rather tense."

"Is it because some of the settlers have been attacked by a bear?" asked Matsuzo.

"So you've heard about the bear," murmured Setona.

"You know that very well," retorted Matsuzo. "I saw you eavesdropping."

Setona suddenly smiled. Despite her exotic features, she was an extraordinarily attractive woman. "I often listen behind the door of my brother's reception room. I learn many useful things that way."

"Y-your brother?" stammered Matsuzo, looking confused.

"My mother was the commander's wet nurse, and he treated her as his real mother and me as his sister," explained Setona. Her lips twisted. "I thought you'd heard the gossip already. The people here talk quite freely about me behind my back."

"So Commander Kato was motherless?" asked Zenta. Setona had seemed to soften when speaking about the commander. There was genuine affection in her voice.

"His mother died in childbirth, and since there

were very few women in the settlement, the people here begged the Ainus to find someone to breast-feed the baby."

"How did your mother happen to be chosen as the commander's wet nurse?" asked Zenta.

"She wasn't chosen; she offered herself!" Setona's eyes flashed and she spoke proudly. "My mother was a headman's daughter, and she was married to a great Ainu hunter."

She fell silent, and Zenta could tell that the subject was painful. After a moment Setona continued. "There was a cruel winter one year, before I was born, and the salmon harvest was disastrous. My mother's baby died, and then her husband was killed in a hunting accident."

"Didn't the Japanese in the settlement here know about the starvation?" asked Zenta. "Couldn't they help?"

"Of course they helped!" said Setona, her voice as bitter as gall. "They gave the Ainus enough millet to keep them from starvation. And in exchange they got a wet nurse for the commander. My mother had just lost her baby, and her breasts were still swollen with milk, so she volunteered herself."

"A wet nurse in exchange for millet," murmured Zenta.

Setona smiled coldly. "The settlers are shrewd

traders. In exchange for valuable furs and lumber, they give lacquer dishes and pieces of cotton cloth. Oh, they're seldom losers, these Japanese settlers!"

Her expression reminded Zenta of Tonkuru's contemptuous reference to the "treasures" they saw on the shelves in the Ainu houses.

"Your mother did not return to her own people after the commander was weaned?" he asked.

Setona's face lost some of its harshness. "My mother had become fond of the baby she nursed, and he loved her too much to let her leave. So as a 'reward' for her services, she was given in marriage to one of the Japanese soldiers here." She added in a low voice, "I am the daughter of that marriage."

She had pride, this woman who was neither wholly Ainu nor wholly Japanese. But there was something very forlorn about her, and Zenta felt a deep sympathy for her. He was an outcast himself, forced to leave home at the age of fifteen. Two years later he had had a parting almost as painful, when he had left a respected teacher. He knew the meaning of loneliness.

Setona might be an anomaly in the settlement, but she was not without power. "Your mother had some influence over Commander Kato, didn't she?" asked Zenta. "He must feel more friendship for the Ainu people because of her."

Setona nodded. "She told him many stories about her people, and he understands the Ainus better than anyone else here."

"So that's why he is so unwilling to go to war with the Ainus," said Matsuzo, "in spite of the strong pressure from his steward."

"I really asked you to come so that I could have news about my mother's village," said Setona. She looked wistful. "How did you find the people? The headman is my uncle, you know, and Ashiri, Tonkuru, and Mopi are my cousins."

"They all looked healthy," began Zenta. He knew that this was not what she wanted to ask about. "Is there anything in particular you want to know?"

Setona bit her lip. "I suppose what I really want to know is how they feel about the Japanese here."

Zenta hesitated. "Opinion seemed divided. The headman and Tonkuru want to stay on good terms with the Japanese settlers. Ashiri seems more hostile. But I can't be sure about this, because he didn't speak any Japanese."

"What about others?" asked Setona. "Did you meet men from outside the headman's family?"

"My guess is that most of Ashiri's friends feel as he does," replied Zenta. "Among the older men I met the headman's brother, the leader of the hunters. Again, because of the language problem, I can't tell you how he feels."

"So as far as you know, Tonkuru and the headman have very few active supporters?" asked Setona.

"I'm sorry, but I don't know the answer," said Zenta. He added quietly, "We saw your cousin Tonkuru just before we arrived here. He asked us to bring a message to you."

Setona stared at him. "What is the message?"

"He said to tell you that he has not given up hope."

She closed her eyes, and her hands clenched tightly. "I see," she said huskily.

She lowered her head and was silent. After a moment, the two men realized that the interview was over. They rose, mumbled a farewell, and left the room. In their last glimpse of Setona, she was still looking down at the floor.

"He loves her, doesn't he?" remarked Matsuzo as the two ronin made their way back to their lodging.

"Tonkuru?" asked Zenta. "Yes, he loves Setona. I suspect she loves him as well."

He thought back to Tonkuru's desolate figure just before he turned away. "Things look pretty hopeless for him. He can't even come to the settlement to visit her, now that there's so much bad feeling against the Ainu people."

Returning to the long wooden building where their lodging was, the two ronin went to their room. But there was no sign of anyone bringing in trays with their evening meal.

"Service is slow here," complained Matsuzo.

Zenta, who had experienced a great many more ups and downs in his life, did not wait passively for his dinner. "I'd better find the kitchen and see what the situation is. Remember what Jimbei said: There is a shortage of women in the settlement. That means the service here may not be what you are used to."

He was right. When Matsuzo followed Zenta to the kitchen, the two ronin found several men gathered around a huge clay stove, helping themselves from a rice bucket and from various dishes standing on a counter. The men sat on the ends of some barrels, which stood on the clay floor of the kitchen, or they simply squatted. When Jimbei had told the two newcomers that there was little ceremony here, thought Matsuzo, he had grossly understated the case.

The men greeted the newcomers cheerfully. "Jimbei told us about you," mumbled one man with his mouth full. "You're just in time. There's still a little food left."

A couple of the men stood up and offered their barrels. "We're almost finished, anyway."

Matsuzo bowed politely and accepted one of the barrels. Conditions in this raw frontier town might be primitive, but the men here were friendly enough. Taking up a rice bowl, he went eagerly to the bucket—and was disappointed to find millet, not rice, inside. Still, it was better than the Ainu fare he had been eating lately. He helped himself greedily to the pickled radishes and pumpkin cooked in soy sauce. He had never properly appreciated what a delicious condiment soy sauce was.

Another treat was in a big iron pot, kept warm over the embers of the charcoal fire. When one of the men lifted the lid to fill his bowl, Matsuzo's nose twitched in ecstasy on catching the deep, rich smell of fermented bean paste. "Miso soup," he sighed, and rushed over to fill his own bowl. Zenta quickly joined him, and for a moment the two ronin simply stared down at the thick brown soup and inhaled its fragrance.

"I see you missed the taste of real, civilized food," remarked one of the men, grinning. "What did those savages feed you, anyway?"

By now Matsuzo was used to hearing the men in the settlement refer to the Ainus as savages, but he still found it annoying. Although he had been shocked by the bloody rites during the Bear Festival, he objected when others called the Ainus savages. They were individuals—he thought of Mopi—and some of the ones he had met were intelligent and sensitive.

But this was no time, decided Matsuzo, to give the men here a lecture on the Ainus. He was too hungry. He glanced at Zenta and saw that his friend was already helping himself to a second bowl of the miso soup.

The questioner still waited for an answer. "We were fed a lot of fish," replied Matsuzo. "It was certainly fresh enough, but it lacked seasoning."

Having finished their first satisfactory meal in weeks, the two ronin retired to their room replete and unwilling to think of anything except bed. Since there was no maidservant, they had to make the beds themselves. Matsuzo did not dare grumble as he unfolded the futon for his bed. He was afraid that he might find the settlement all a dream, and he would wake up again under a scratchy cover in Ashiri's house.

The settlement was no dream. Matsuzo woke up and found himself still under a soft, cotton-filled quilt. Breakfast was simpler than last night's dinner, but it was still a pleasure to use chopsticks and eat broiled salted fish. His main complaint about Ainu food was not the exotic ingredients but its blandness.

Jimbei arrived just as they were finishing breakfast and offered to take them on a tour of the settlement. There was not very much to see, since the place was little more than a village, fenced for protection.

The two ronin spent most of their day answering questions. Many people had heard of the two men's arrival, and came to ask them about the Ainus. The settlers thought it a terrible ordeal to have spent a whole week with the savages, and Matsuzo became embarrassed when people congratulated him on having survived the experience. Both men protested that their Ainu hosts were gentle, even gracious, but Matsuzo could see that few of their listeners believed them.

"It's been decided that you will be working on the moat," Jimbei told the two newcomers that evening. "That's the most important project at the moment, and manpower is needed there. I'll show you the site, and you can start work first thing tomorrow morning."

"You feel that a strong defense is necessary here?" asked Zenta as they went outside the fence that surrounded the settlement.

"That feeling has been growing," said Jimbei. "Ever since the bear attacks began, the people here want as much protection as possible around their homes."

"Won't the fence alone keep out the bear?" asked Zenta. He put his hands around one of the tree trunks used to form the wooden fence and shook it. "It seems pretty stout to me. You can't break through this fence without tools, and bears don't use tools."

"But *men* do," said Jimbei. It wasn't necessary to ask him what he meant.

Standing outside the fence, they looked around. A wide stretch of ground had been cleared of trees and leveled. In one place a deep ditch was being dug, forming the beginnings of a moat. That, too, seemed like a defense not against bears, but against men.

It was bitterly cold, and the ground was so hard that their steps had a metallic ring. No wonder the work was going so slowly, thought Matsuzo. It would be like digging through rock, and he did not look forward to starting work the next day.

On the main island of Japan spring was around the corner, and in some places the plum trees were already in bloom. At this time of the year, Matsuzo thought wistfully, he would normally be writing poems to the fragrant white blossoms. But the land was still in the grip of winter here in the north, and he would be digging ditches.

Back inside the fence Jimbei accompanied the two ronin to their lodging, and as they walked, he asked them questions about the customs of the Ainus. So far he was the only person Matsuzo had met who was curious about how the natives lived, what their houses were like, and how they gathered food. All the other people he had talked with were more concerned with the Ainus' capacity for war—even the commander, although he didn't seem totally convinced that war was inevitable. Jimbei was also the only person who had come really close to the Ainu village.

"You know, if they weren't so ugly, I might like to get acquainted with one of these curious people," he said thoughtfully. "We could learn a few things from them—how to live in this cold country, for instance."

"Appearance is the easiest thing to get used to," said Matsuzo. "After a day or two, I didn't think about their funny eyes anymore, or even the women's tattoos. What bothered me were some of their customs." He was thinking of the Bear Festival.

The three men arrived at the long wooden building where the newcomers were staying, and they were just about to enter when they heard cries behind them.

"The bear!" someone screamed. "It's inside the settlement!"

They ran back toward the gate and halted at the sight in front of them. A huge, shaggy figure was standing with its back to them and shaking a bundle of rags. The bundle turned out to be a man, already unconscious, whose head and limbs flopped limply. A number of people cowered in doorways nearby.

"Get me some ropes!" Zenta told Jimbei. "Make sure they're strong and at least ten feet long, preferably twenty."

"But . . . but . . ." began Jimbei.

"There's no time to waste!" snapped Zenta.

Matsuzo guessed what Zenta was planning to do. "We need more people," he whispered, and swallowed. "Back at the festival they had nearly a dozen men, and the bear was only a cub. This one is fully grown!"

"Well, we can't feed it berries and acorns!"

The huge, shaggy figure growled and turned around. The light was failing fast, but Matsuzo thought he saw teeth: big, sharp teeth.

Jimbei came rushing back with several pieces of rope. "What are you going to do?" he asked Zenta.

Without answering, Zenta fashioned the end of one rope into a noose. Matsuzo quickly followed his example, and after a moment's hesitation Jimbei took up a piece of rope as well.

Zenta's noose was ready, and he cast it around the neck of the beast. It didn't seem to notice, and continued to shake its victim.

Matsuzo threw his noose and missed. He tried again and finally succeeded in getting it around the bear's neck. Jimbei threw several times without success. After trying again and again, he finally got it over the head of the beast.

Zenta looked around. "We need as many men as possible," he told the people shivering in the doorways. No volunteers came forward—not that Matsuzo could blame them.

"Very well then," said Zenta, and turned to his two assistants. "Now pull!"

Unlike the ropes used by the Ainus during their festival, which were intended to control the movement of the bear, Zenta's had been formed into a slip knot, a noose intended to choke. Matsuzo had followed his example in constructing his noose.

At first the bear hardly noticed and continued to shake his limp victim. But when Matsuzo gave a hard tug, the bear turned its head. Matsuzo found himself staring straight into its eyes. He was so struck by the viciousness in those eyes that he nearly let go of the rope. He recovered just in time and grasped the rope firmly as the bear suddenly lunged.

The three men holding the ropes could not prevent the bear from dragging them after it as it lurched back and forth. Panting and gasping with effort, Matsuzo found it hard even to stay on his feet.

"Pull!" cried Zenta.

Matsuzo pulled. A human being with three nooses tight around his neck would have been well strangled by now, but the bear was only maddened. Horrible grunts came from its throat, and Matsuzo could feel its hot, fetid breath on his face.

But at least the bear, in its struggles against the ropes, had dropped its victim. None of them could spare the time to see if the man had been badly injured.

Matsuzo realized that the grunting sounds coming from the bear were familiar. He had heard them before, during the Ainu Bear Festival. Without even realizing it, he began to repeat the shouts he had heard from the crowd at the festival.

The effect of his shouting was immediate: The bear suddenly froze. Then, with a mighty jerk, it tore the ropes from the hands of the three men. Matsuzo hissed with pain as the rope whipped through his hands, scraping the skin from his palms.

Before the three men could recover, the bear turned and lumbered through the open gate, dragging the pieces of rope behind it.

"Let it go," gasped Zenta, rushing over to the gate and shutting it. He pushed the stout horizontal crosspiece into place.

Matsuzo limped over to the gate and peered at the retreating figure of the bear. Zenta pulled him back. "You're welcome to chase after the bear if you want," he panted, "but I'm through for the night."

For some minutes they stood trying to catch their breath. "You'll have to teach me those shouts, the ones that made the bear run off like that," said Jimbei when he could speak again. "Where did you learn them? From the Ainus?"

"Yes, but don't ask me what they mean," said Matsuzo. "We heard the Ainus giving these shouts during one of their festivals. Maybe they reminded the bear of something unpleasant."

Groans were coming from the victim of the bear. Now that the danger was over, several of the people in the doorways ventured out. The doctor who had tended Matsuzo's leg was summoned, and he bent down. "His chest is badly mauled, but no bones seem to be broken. I think he must have fainted."

The injured man moaned and opened his eyes. "Is it gone?" he whispered.

"Yes, it's gone. You're safe now."

Zenta walked over to the injured man. "Can you tell us what happened?"

Someone brought over a cup of water. The injured man drank a little, but his hands shook so badly that he spilled most of the water. He waved the cup away. "I was walking by the gate and noticed that it was standing open. I went over to see if someone was still outside. Then a huge, black thing grabbed me and shook me until my teeth rattled in my head. I don't remember anything more."

"Who was the last person to. go outside the fence tonight?" demanded one of the men. "He's the one who is guilty of leaving the gate open! He should be severely punished for his carelessness!"

They all looked at one another, but no one admitted to having gone out. Jimbei had taken the two newcomers out to look at the moat, but after they had returned, he had closed the gate. Or had he? Matsuzo tried to remember which of them had been the last to pass through.

Had anyone gone out after they had returned and then carelessly left the gate open? Or *was* it carelessness?

EIGHT

During their last interview with Commander Kato, the only other person officially present had been the steward. Now the room was crowded. In addition to the two ronin and Jimbei, there were several witnesses to the bear attack. Even the victim of the attack was there, bandaged and still badly shaken.

The frown line was visible between the steward's eyes, but now he looked curiously satisfied, even triumphant. He also regarded the two newcomers with respect. He thought we were just two extra mouths to feed, thought Matsuzo, and two extra pairs of hands for digging ditches.

"It seems you learned some useful tricks while

staying with the savages," the steward said to the two ronin.

"They weren't just useful tricks," objected the commander. "They were the actions of two very brave men." He glanced around and noticed Jimbei. "Three brave men."

There were murmurs of agreement from the others in the room. "Without their help, I would have been torn to pieces!" said the victim of the attack in a hoarse, shaky voice.

"Never mind that," said the steward. "What we have to find out is exactly what happened. Did you do anything to provoke the bear?"

The victim shrank back under the steward's frowning gaze. "N-no! I just walked up to the gate, and the bear pushed his way in and grabbed me. I didn't do anything!"

Commander Kato put his hand over his mouth to stifle a yawn. He was in his white sleeping robe, with a padded kimono thrown over his shoulders. It was very late, and he had obviously been roused from bed. "I think we should stop persecuting this poor man and let him go home," he said. "After all, it wasn't *his* fault that he got mauled."

"I wasn't trying to persecute the man!" protested the steward. He took a deep breath, obviously struggling for patience. "I was trying to find out why a bear, which normally hibernates at this time of the year, should come to the settlement and attack one of our people!"

"We'd spend our time more profitably in trying to find out why the gate was open," remarked the commander. He rocked back and forth a few times. "Someone has been criminally careless."

It certainly took them long enough to come to this point, thought Matsuzo. "Who went outside the gate after we did?" he asked.

There was a long silence. The men in the room looked at one another, but no one spoke up. Jimbei shifted uneasily. "You live near the gate, don't you?" he said to one of the witnesses. "Didn't you see anyone go out after the three of us came back?"

The man shook his head. "It was awfully cold, and I didn't stir out of my house until I heard the screaming."

"Forget about the gate!" cried the steward. "The important thing is that our people are in danger and we must protect them!"

"What can we do that we haven't done already?" objected the commander. A faint whine came into his voice. "You've already got all our able-bodied men digging that miserable moat!"

"A moat is only for defense," the steward said grimly. "We must take the offense."

So this is it, thought Matsuzo. The steward wants war with the Ainus, and now he has an excuse for starting it.

Commander Kato pulled his quilted kimono closer around his shoulders. "We've gone over this argument before. In the first place, I'm not convinced that the Ainus are responsible for the bear. In the second place, I'm not sure we can win a war against them."

"Ah, but things are different now," said the steward. "Because we have the help of our two newcomers, who not only know something about the ways of the Ainus but also have some skill in managing bears."

Everyone turned to look at the two ronin. "Well?" asked the steward. "Do you think we can win a war against the Ainus?"

Zenta was silent. Finally he raised his head. "Not easily. The Ainus are brave people."

The steward stiffened with outrage. "The Japanese samurai are the bravest fighting men in the world! As a member of that class yourself, you should be ashamed!"

Zenta did not look in the least cowed. "They also have powerful weapons," he murmured.

"The samurai sword is supreme," the steward said angrily. "Moreover, our bows have a far greater range than theirs. We can shoot down those savages long before we come into the range of their arrows."

"And yet there is an Ainu legend about a god called Okikumuri who uses the long bow," said Zenta. "How do we know the Ainus themselves don't practice with it as well?"

Matsuzo turned and stared at his friend. What was Zenta trying to do? He knew perfectly well the Ainus didn't have the long bow. That was the very reason they had mistaken him for a god when he shot down the gull.

"That's right!" said the commander. "My foster mother told me stories about this god Okikumuri. Some say he's identified with our own hero, Yoshitsune, who is rumored to have settled in these parts."

"Enough of these fairy tales!" said the steward, then reddened as he realized that he was scolding his own superior. Recovering, he said stiffly, "I'm sorry, my lord. I was speaking to this ronin, who is filling our ears with nonsense. I suggest that we think over very seriously the possibility of launching an attack on those savages—before they attack us first."

The commander yawned. "Fine. Let's think over very seriously the possibility. And now why don't we all go to bed?"

———

135

The steward is set on starting a war, thought Matsuzo as they walked back to their lodging. The commander is opposed to war, that is equally clear. Is he strong enough to oppose his determined steward?

Jimbei was walking back with them. Since the struggle with the bear, he seemed reluctant to leave the company of the two ronin. "I don't think anybody will mind if you don't join the ditchdiggers tomorrow morning," he said. "You've earned your rest."

"I'm glad," said Matsuzo, and he meant it. He looked at Zenta, who had not said a word since they had left the commander's residence. "Do you think we should start giving lessons on throwing rope?"

Zenta merely grunted without saying a word. Looking at his friend's set face, Matsuzo recognized one of Zenta's black moods. It was useless speaking to him.

He turned back to Jimbei. "How do most of the people here feel about a war with the Ainus?"

Jimbei thought for a moment. "I think most people want to avoid trouble with the natives as much as possible. After all, the Ainus know the country, as you pointed out. We'd be at a definite disadvantage. But if they keep sending bears here to attack us, we'll have to do something. We can't allow ourselves to be killed or mutilated one by one."

Zenta broke his silence. "Why do you think the Ainus are responsible for *sending* the bear here? It's true they keep some bears in captivity, but they're cubs. The bear we saw tonight was fully grown."

"It may have been a fully grown bear, but it responded to the Ainu cries I made," Matsuzo said. "That means it must have had some contact with the Ainu people."

It was a good point, and Zenta nodded. "You're right. I wondered about that."

They had arrived at their lodging, but in spite of the late hour, Jimbei was obviously still reluctant to leave them. "The natives are trying to drive us out of Ezo and back to the mainland. I'm sure of it."

"There's plenty of room for everybody," said Matsuzo. "Some of the Ainus seem willing to share the land with the settlers." He was thinking of Tonkuru.

"Yes, but they believe that we ruin the land when we raise crops," said Jimbei. He sounded aggrieved.

"But we do, don't we?" said Zenta. "After we till the land and plant crops, their women can no longer gather wild foodstuffs there."

"Yes, but planting crops is a much more efficient use of land!" protested Jimbei. His cheeks showed no sign of dimples, and for once he looked completely serious. "With our agricultural methods, we can feed many more people. We're bringing civilization to the island."

Zenta slid open the front door with its ugly scraping noise. "Maybe the Ainus are not grateful."

"Then that proves they're savages!" said Jimbei. "In the time of our commander's father, some of the nearby Ainu villages were very hard hit during a disastrous salmon season. If we hadn't given them grain, all the Ainus in those villages would have starved to death. You'd think they *would* be grateful and try to learn how to plant crops, instead of sending bears to attack us!"

Matsuzo found himself agreeing with Jimbei, although he didn't say so aloud. Zenta was still looking moody.

Jimbei reluctantly took leave of them, and the two ronin went silently to their room. The house was quiet, for everyone else had long since retired. They began to unfold some futons for their beds. "On the mainland even the poorest inn would have a maid to make our beds," grumbled Matsuzo once again. But he lay down with a contented sigh.

Matsuzo was nearly asleep when he heard Zenta's voice. "I'm going back to the Ainu village."

Matsuzo thought he had not heard properly. He sat up. "What did you say?"

"I can't take part in a war against the Ainus," said Zenta. His voice was soft but resolute. "I have to go back and warn the headman about the plans to attack them."

"You can't mean it!" Matsuzo was almost gibbering. "You want to go back and stay with those savages again?" The word just slipped out.

"Those savages, as you call them, saved our lives." Zenta's voice was no longer soft, but stung like a whip. "They fed us with food they could ill afford to spare. I owe them a debt, and I intend to repay it."

"But the people here have also fed us and treated us well!" cried Matsuzo. He took a deep breath and tried to keep his voice down. "Don't we owe *them* anything? They're being attacked by a bear, almost certainly sent by the Ainus. It's only right that we should help them to defend themselves."

"You're forgetting the gate," said Zenta. "Someone inside the settlement left that gate open."

"What does that have to do with it?" cried Matsuzo. "The Ainu sent the bear to attack the settlement, and we have to protect it!"

139

"Someone inside *wanted* the bear to enter, knowing that would inflame feelings here and start a war."

"If that's true," muttered Matsuzo, "his intentions are good. He wants to protect the settlement."

"Perhaps the Ainus, too, want to protect their kotans," said Zenta. "Don't you see, I want to learn the truth! I want to find out why the bear is attacking people here, and who is responsible for it. Some of the Ainus do want to live in peace with the Japanese settlers, and I have to tell them that the Japanese believe the bear was deliberately sent!"

Matsuzo wanted to weep. "But how can we desert our own people? We'd be leaving a civilized society and going back to people who eat with their hands and tattoo their lips!"

"You stayed with those people for more than a week and didn't find life there so intolerable. Mopi tended your wounded leg."

"I can't bring myself to go back," said Matsuzo, ignoring Zenta's last remark. "I can't face the smell inside their houses, the unwashed bodies. I can't face their barbarous rites, the sacrifice of live animals."

"You don't have to go," said Zenta. "I'm quite ready to go alone."

Matsuzo was shocked into silence. During the year he had traveled in Zenta's company, he had considered himself the other man's follower and had respected his authority. This time he was unable to accept Zenta's judgment. How could he go against his own people and ally himself with those whose customs, practices, and beliefs were so alien and repulsive?

On a few occasions Matsuzo had been able to coax Zenta out of some rash course of action. But now, looking at the expression on his friend's face, he knew it was hopeless.

Matsuzo swallowed hard. "When do you plan to leave?"

"As soon as there is light enough to travel," said Zenta. He must have heard the rejection in Matsuzo's voice, but he gave no sign. He blew out the wick in their oil lamp and lay down on his bed. A taut silence hung over the darkened room.

Matsuzo's breathing was shallow and fast. He tried to whip himself into anger, because anger could fend off sorrow. How could Zenta go away and abandon these settlers? How could Zenta abandon *him*? They were Japanese, a people beleaguered in a hostile land. The settlers were surrounded by marauding animals that attacked innocent children. They needed help. Instead, Zenta intended to go and help their enemies.

141

Matsuzo had never been so desperately unhappy as during the small hours of that bitter winter morning. Time dragged on agonizingly slowly, and yet he didn't want to see the daylight arrive.

Somehow, he must have dozed off. He awoke to the sound of rustling cloth, and saw that Zenta was standing up and adjusting the sash of his kimono. Since Zenta could move as silently as a cat, he must have made the rustling noise deliberately. It was now bright enough for them to see each other's faces.

"If a war does not break out between the Ainus and the settlers, perhaps we can meet here again," Zenta said. He spoke quietly, without reproach. In the next instant he was gone.

Matsuzo jumped up and ran to the door. There were a dozen things he wanted to say. He thought about Zenta's spells of black depression, when he hardly bothered to stir himself to eat. Who would care for him now? Watch out for hidden spring bows, Matsuzo wanted to say. Don't talk to strange bears. Try not to stab your foot when spearing fish.

He said nothing, and stood biting his lip until he could taste blood.

Outside, the cold hit Zenta's face like a blow. He looked around and saw no one in the street. It was too early and too cold for anyone to venture out. After the fracas with the bear, he almost expected to see a guard posted at the gate, but even there he met no one.

Once through the gate, he walked quickly past the cleared area until he came to some trees. In the shelter of the trees, he performed a necessary but distasteful task: taking off his clothes and replacing them with the dirty Ainu garments he had kept and brought with him. He was shuddering by the time he finally finished dressing himself in the coarsely woven robe, fur cloak, and deerskin boots—and it was not only from the cold.

It was time to make for the Ainu kotan. He was almost certain he remembered the way, but things might look different now that he was going in the opposite direction. As he walked, he thought over and over again about his decision to leave. The break with Matsuzo had been much harder than he had expected.

True, his life had prepared him for painful breaks. His ten years of ceaseless wandering had made him hardy, and prepared him for friendships that had to be broken off.

And yet it had been a surprisingly hard wrench to turn away from Matsuzo and walk out of that lodging house. Perhaps Matsuzo had taken the place of the younger brother whom he had sworn never to see again. Perhaps that was why he had not taken Jimbei's map with him. He was still hoping that Matsuzo would change his mind and use the map to follow him back to the Ainu village. But of course that was a vain hope.

He understood perfectly well why Matsuzo had refused to return to the Ainu village. It wasn't because of the unfamiliar food, the rough clothing, or the unwashed bodies. It was the Bear Festival, and the sight of Mopi laughing with glee during the bloody sacrifices.

Zenta himself had been nauseated by the sight. But he had to return to the Ainus. They had saved his life, and he had to warn them of a plot to incriminate them, to make it seem that they had deliberately sent the vicious bear. Whether the plot had been devised by the war-mongering steward or by some other person, the Japanese settlers were in the mood to mount an attack.

Zenta couldn't forget the face of Setona, so proud and yet so sad. If war should break out between the Japanese and the Ainus, she would never see Tonkuru again.

Despite Zenta's preoccupation, his training kept his senses alert. The sound of two bare branches rubbing against each other was normal. The crackle of ice on the surface of the stream was a sign of approaching spring. What finally caught his ear and sent a warning was the faint squeak of a foot carefully pressing down on powdery snow.

Had Matsuzo changed his mind and decided to come after all? But he would not be walking so cautiously, so stealthily. This footstep had been made by someone who did not want to be heard.

Hitching his fur cloak to hide his movement, Zenta reached his hand inside and loosened his sword in its scabbard. He also undid the draw-string of his cloak.

The attack was fast. There was a flurry of steps, and Zenta flung himself aside just in time to avoid the vicious thrust of a spear. As he whirled around, he drew his sword with one hand and with the other hand flung his cloak into the face of his attacker.

As the attacker struggled with the cloak, Zenta seized the shaft of the spear and, with a sharp wrench, tore it out of the other man's hands.

The face emerging from the folds of the fur cloak was that of a stranger, a Japanese settler.

"Why did you attack me?" demanded Zenta.

Panting, the settler nursed his wrist and then stared at Zenta's glittering sword. "You are a traitor!" he spat. "You desert your own people to join forces with the enemy."

Seeing the hatred in the settler's eyes, Zenta knew it was useless to try to change the man's mind. He was more interested in finding out how the attacker happened to be stalking him. "Who sent you?" he asked.

Whether from pain, from hatred, or from cold, the settler began to shiver violently. "I won't tell! You can kill me if you wish!"

Zenta decided he was wasting valuable time. He flung the spear away, deep into the trees. "Very well, then. Go back and tell whoever sent you that I'm not joining forces with our enemy. Instead, I am trying to find out just who our enemy is."

He picked up his cloak and began to walk away. Behind him he heard the other man step forward, hesitate, and then walk back in the direction of the settlement.

Someone in the settlement had been spying on him, thought Zenta, and had seen him go outside the gate. That same person had decided to send an assassin after him. Was it the same man who had left the gate open for the bear?

Soon he reached the place where the small stream joined the river. It was near here Matsuzo had said that he had seen a bear. At the time Zenta had doubted the sighting. But now, having had an actual encounter with a real bear, he admitted that Matsuzo's eyes had not deceived him. Was it the same bear? Could there be two bears at large, at a time when they should all be hibernating?

He felt a moment's indecision over which direction to go next. Had they always had the stream on their right hand, or had they crossed the stream at one point, where the ice was solid? No, he remembered: The stream had always been on their right, which meant he should turn this way. . . .

The moment's hesitation saved his life. While looking around, he noticed that some dozen paces ahead of him, a snowy patch of ground reflected the morning light in a different way from the area surrounding it. There were signs of human handiwork here.

Zenta held his breath and walked forward gingerly, scrutinizing every bit of ground before putting his foot down. Then he saw it. Nearly invisible on the ground was a ridge of snow, about the thickness of a finger. He knew exactly what was inside: a cord, attached to the trigger of a spring bow. If he had followed the stream as he had intended, his foot would have brushed against the cord and released the arrow. And the arrow would be poisoned with aconite.

He was definitely back in Ainu territory.

Carefully skirting the stretch of ground with its deadly trap, he brushed his way past bushes and scrub bamboo, dislodging snow as he went. Undoubtedly, his noisy passage would be noticed by all the Ainus in the vicinity. Perhaps they already knew of his coming, even before this. Their ears were keener than his, at least in their home territory.

But how would they receive him?

As the path turned around a clump of pine trees, he had his answer. Waiting for him were Ashiri and two of his friends. They all held bows fitted with arrows, and all three arrows were pointed in his direction.

NINE

He could cut down one of the men, thought Zenta, before an arrow hit him. Once he was struck by an arrow, he might even be able to kill another man, if the effect of the poison was not immediate. But that still left one more man, and by then he might be so weakened by the aconite that the last man could dispatch him easily.

No, the chances of surviving a fight with the three Ainu men were poor. Not only would he go to his death, but the death would be pointless, and he would have failed in his task.

Zenta came to a decision. Slowly, keeping his hands always in sight, he took out his two swords and laid them on the ground. Then he retreated a step and waited with his arms folded.

Even without a common language, the meaning of his gesture was unmistakable. He tried to keep his face impassive, but he felt a trickle of perspiration run down his back. He studied the expression on Ashiri's face.

Ashiri was scowling, but that was normal. Sullenness seemed to be his second nature. Was he much more angry than usual? Whatever Ashiri decided to do, the other two men would follow him, for he was obviously their leader.

Ashiri finally broke his silence. He turned to one of the men and barked out an order. Amid the rapid string of Ainu words he heard, Zenta picked out one that he knew: Tonkuru. He felt a vast relief. They were going to give him a chance to explain.

After the man rushed off on his errand, one of the others made a move to pick up Zenta's swords. Again Ashiri barked out an order, and the man quickly retreated. This was another good sign.

Ashiri looked briefly at Zenta, and then kicked the two swords toward him.

Zenta stiffened, and a red-hot rage filled his head, like molten iron. A samurai's sword was his soul, and to treat a man's sword contemptuously by kicking it was an insult that could be wiped out only with blood.

On an intellectual level he knew that customs were different here, and that Ashiri did not understand the significance of his gesture. Nevertheless it took all of Zenta's willpower to control his anger.

He told himself that Ashiri was actually saying, without words, that Zenta's weapons had not been confiscated—yet. But the air between them still crackled with tension. Perhaps Ashiri had an inkling of Zenta's momentary rage.

The tension broke with the sound of running footsteps. Tonkuru rushed up panting and stared at Zenta. "I was told that you were back, but I didn't believe it." A slow grin passed over his face. "Don't tell me that you miss our cooking?"

Zenta felt himself relaxing and he grinned back. He bent down and, with hands still trembling a little, picked up his swords. He hadn't realized until now how much he liked the man. "Yes, I missed especially the salmon stewed with wild garlic."

Tonkuru stopped smiling. "But your friend has not returned. He is not equally fond of our food? Or of our other customs?"

It was useless to lie. "No, he is not," admitted Zenta. "I came back alone because I have some

151

very serious news to tell you."

"I see that you have," said Tonkuru, his face becoming grave. "You had better speak to my father and my uncle."

In the headman's house the room soon became crowded as his brother, the hunter, arrived with some of his followers. Ashiri and his friends squeezed into the room as well.

With Tonkuru acting as translator, Zenta described the savage bear attack on the settler. He added that the Japanese had suffered a number of such attacks, and that one of the victims was the compound's only child, a young boy, who had been badly mauled.

A buzz of comments ran through the room when he finished. Tonkuru's uncle, the hunter, raised his voice.

"He says that you must have been mistaken," translated Tonkuru. "Bears are supposed to be hibernating at this time of the year."

"I was not mistaken," said Zenta. "The animal I encountered was most certainly a bear."

The hunter, smiling skeptically, asked a question. "He wants to know if it could have been a tall and powerful man, dressed in a bear skin," translated Tonkuru.

Zenta remembered the violence of his own struggles while pulling the rope around the neck of the beast. "No. No human could have been that powerful."

Then he thought of something. "Could one of your captive bear cubs have escaped within the last few years? Captivity could have upset its natural rhythm and its instinct to hibernate."

Tonkuru required a little time to translate Zenta's suggestion. When he had finished, there was a thoughtful silence. It was the headman who answered, and Tonkuru became excited as well. He finally turned to Zenta. "During our Bear Festival two years ago, one of our sacrificial cubs did escape. We never recaptured it."

"Then the rogue bear could be this missing cub!" suggested Zenta. "Something has made it turn against the people of the settlement. When we were struggling with the bear, my friend gave some of the same shouts he had heard during your Bear Festival. The bear reacted to the shouts and ran off. Perhaps it remembered those shouts because you had already wounded it before it managed to escape."

A babble broke out when Tonkuru translated Zenta's suggestion. The hunter's voice cut through the noise. "Are you implying that our people have deliberately trained a bear to attack the Japanese settlers?" translated Tonkuru.

"No, that is not what *I* am implying," replied

Zenta. "But many of the settlers do believe it, and they're talking about going to war against you. This is what I came to tell you. This is why I returned."

Tonkuru translated and the room exploded with angry shouts. Finally the headman stood up. By the sheer force of his presence, he quieted the room, even his son Ashiri, the angriest and loudest of the young men.

The headman looked at Zenta for a moment and spoke. "We thank you for bringing us this warning, so that we have time to strengthen our defenses," said Tonkuru, translating. "We must hunt down this rogue bear, if what you say is true. Such a beast is dangerous to everyone, and it is our task to discover why it is behaving in this unnatural way."

Zenta bowed. He had delivered his warning, and it was being taken seriously. The meeting broke into smaller groups, and the headman approached his brother, the most skillful hunter of the clan. Zenta guessed that the hunter was being asked to track down the rogue bear.

Tonkuru beckoned to Zenta, and the two of them went outside, where they were able to converse quietly, away from the noise.

"What will you do if war should break out between our people and the settlers?" asked the young Ainu. "Can you bring yourself to fight your own countrymen?"

Zenta had already asked himself the question during the bleak predawn hours with Matsuzo in their lodging house at the settlement. "I owe your people too much to fight you, but neither can I fight my own people. I'll take up arms only to separate the combatants—and to prevent hostilities, if I possibly can."

Before Tonkuru could reply, Ashiri came storming out of the door. Ashiri asked his brother a question, and when he received Tonkuru's quiet answer, he curled his lips and spat some words.

One of Ashiri's friends added some jeering remark, and Zenta heard the name Setona. Tonkuru had the fair complexion of his people, but now he turned even whiter. He managed to control himself and answered with dignity.

Ashiri snapped at the man who had jeered at Tonkuru, and then he stamped off toward his own house, followed by his friends.

Tonkuru stood looking after his brother. Younger than any of the others at the meeting, he nevertheless carried himself like a leader.

"I did have a chance to meet Setona," Zenta told the young Ainu. "I gave her your message."

Tonkuru caught his breath. "What did she say?"

Zenta remembered the way the young woman

had clenched her hands. "She said very little, but I think she was deeply affected."

"We . . . we have an understanding," said Tonkuru. His voice was not quite steady. "I used to go to the settlement regularly, when we still had good relations with the Japanese. At first I visited her because she was my cousin." He turned to look at Zenta. "Did you know that her mother was my aunt?"

"Yes, she told me that."

"Her Japanese is perfect," said Tonkuru, "and she taught me a little."

"She taught you well," murmured Zenta.

Tonkuru sighed. "Then things started to go wrong. The Japanese settlers wanted more and more land, which our people were reluctant to give them. So they just took it!"

His deep-set eyes flashed. This quiet young man could be formidable, Zenta realized. "What did your people do?" he asked.

"It was Ashiri's idea," said Tonkuru, and he smiled. "He and his friends drove some deer into the settlers' newly planted fields. They ruined nearly a whole season's millet crop."

"I can see that this would annoy a few people," remarked Zenta. He remembered something Jimbei had said and couldn't resist a jab. "But you don't despise millet entirely, do you? Didn't your people receive some millet from the settlers one year, when your salmon harvest was disastrous and the clan faced starvation?"

The smile disappeared from Tonkuru's face. "We have not forgotten that incident. That is why my father works so hard to preserve the peace between our people and the Japanese."

"You agree with your father, then?" asked Zenta.

"Yes," said Tonkuru tightly. "As you see, my brother and his friends despise me for it."

Zenta remembered the jeering mention of Setona by one of Ashiri's followers. The man must have accused Tonkuru of favoring peace with the Japanese because he was in love with Setona.

Zenta was invited to stay at the headman's house after the meeting. He guessed that Okera would be relieved that she didn't have to have him as a guest. With her secret activities at night, she probably wanted few witnesses around.

Zenta suspected that the headman had another reason for inviting him. Ashiri and his friends had probably been given instructions to prepare a defense against a Japanese attack. If that was the case, they would not want their Japanese guest seeing what the defenses would be. His hosts were courteous, Zenta thought ruefully, but they didn't trust him completely.

After sitting down cross-legged in front of the

sunken fireplace, he felt a tug on his sleeve, and turned to see Mopi looking at him. "Your friend not back?" she asked.

Zenta wanted to spare her feelings. "No, he's too busy."

But she was not deceived. "He angry with me," she said in a low voice. "I did something wrong?"

With her small face and huge, round eyes, she reminded him of a kitten who did not understand why it had been scolded. Zenta felt very sorry for her. "*You* didn't do anything wrong. He just wanted to stay with his people at the Japanese settlement." He knew, however, that she was hurt.

Matsuzo wondered how long it would take before the settlers discovered Zenta's departure. He wasn't left to wonder long. Much sooner than he expected, he heard loud voices outside the lodging house and then the sound of stamping feet approaching his room. The door slid open so violently that it almost jumped out of its groove.

Four men stood outside; three of them he remembered as guards at the commander's residence. The fourth man was Jimbei, who hung back from the others. "Where is your friend?" demanded the one who seemed to be the leader.

It was pointless to lie. "He has gone back to the village of the Ainus," replied Matsuzo, wondering how these men had learned about Zenta's departure so quickly.

The men looked at one another. "So it's true," muttered one man.

"Why didn't you go with him?" asked the leader.

Again Matsuzo told the simple truth. "I thought my place was here, with my own people."

The leader looked skeptical. "Then why didn't you stop your friend from leaving?"

Matsuzo stared. "You mean that *I* should try to stop Zenta? Why didn't you try it yourself?"

Again the men looked at one another. "I think Tarobei did go out to look for him," said one of the men. "But he came back and said he was too late and found no traces of the man. Tarobei came back nursing a sprained wrist, though."

Despite his unhappiness, Matsuzo felt a spurt of satisfaction. "It seems that your man Tarobei must have caught up with Zenta after all."

"I shall have to report back to the steward," said the leader. He frowned darkly at Matsuzo. "Don't try to leave this house without permission."

Three of the men left, but Jimbei did not. He sidled into the room and sat down on Matsuzo's pile of folded quilts. After a moment he raised his eyes and looked at Matsuzo. "Do you know exactly why your friend left? He suspects something, doesn't he?"

Matsuzo was suddenly overcome with confusion. Had he forgotten something important? "Zenta said he was not satisfied about the bear that was attacking the people here," he said slowly.

Jimbei let his breath out. "I think I know! He suspects that the gate was *deliberately* left open for the bear, doesn't he?"

Matsuzo now remembered. It was true that Zenta had mentioned the gate before he left.

Jimbei was looking very thoughtful. "You know, a war with the Ainus may not be too easy to win. Whoever left the gate open, I wonder if he realizes that."

"So you agree with Zenta—you think that one of the settlers here deliberately left the gate open," Matsuzo said slowly. "Someone who wants to start a war with the Ainus."

Intent on their thoughts, both men jumped when the door suddenly slid open. "My mistress asks you to visit her," said a voice.

Matsuzo recognized the man who stood in the doorway. He was the one who had brought him and Zenta to Setona two days before. "I'm not supposed to leave this house," he said to the messenger.

"Don't worry about that," Jimbei told Matsuzo. "You'd better obey Setona's order and go with

160

him. She will put you right with the commander's men."

Seeing Setona for the second time, Matsuzo no longer found her appearance quite so exotic. Given time, he might find her beautiful, with her unusually white skin and her delicate features. He could even get used to her deep, round eyes.

Those eyes were now examining him intently. "I understand that your friend has gone back to the Ainu kotan," she said.

Her lips trembled, and he realized that she was under emotional strain. Did she long for her mother's people? Or was she pining for Tonkuru?

"Why did he go back?" she asked softly.

"Zenta was not convinced that the bear that attacked the people here had been sent by the Ainus. So he went to find out more about the animal."

She became completely still. Finally she let out her breath slowly. "He suspects one of the Japanese here? But why should anyone want to do this?" Before Matsuzo could answer, she spoke again. "Yes, of course. Someone wants to start a war. Someone wants to force the hand of the commander, who is reluctant to attack the Ainus."

Matsuzo was ashamed. Both Setona and Jimbei seemed to agree with Zenta, whereas he himself, Zenta's friend, had jumped to the conclusion that the Ainus had sent the vicious bear. Matsuzo now knew why he had been so ready to believe in the Ainus' guilt: He couldn't face the prospect of having to go back to them.

But wait. If someone here was responsible for bringing in the bear, it was his duty to find out who it was and expose him. Then he could help prevent a war—a war which could be costly and could devastate both the settlement and the Ainus. Zenta was working for the same thing, so this meant that he and Zenta were on the same side after all! The heavy weight that had been oppressing Matsuzo suddenly lifted, and his spirits rose.

Setona's soft voice brought Matsuzo down to earth again. "We should not announce our suspicions too loudly," she said. "There are men here who would stop at nothing to gain their ends. If they can bring in a bear to attack people, they would not hesitate to silence you."

Matsuzo knew that she was right, although in his joy he felt himself the equal of a dozen attackers. "Yes, of course," he said quickly. "But we should tell the commander at least. He would agree with us immediately."

"I can speak to him," she said calmly. "He listens to me."

Matsuzo did not doubt her. Setona was the commander's foster sister, almost a member of his family.

"Meanwhile, I'll do what I can to find out who brought in the bear," he promised, and rose to take his leave.

"Fighting the Ainus will be harder than they think," she murmured. This was also Jimbei's opinion, but Setona's expression was different. Her eyes glittered, and Matsuzo realized that she was deeply proud of her mother's people.

"They are very skilled bowmen," he agreed. "And they know the country well."

"They have a god, Okikumuri, who will defend them against their enemies," she said, almost in a singsong voice. Then she looked at him directly, and her voice became normal again. "Perhaps there's some truth in it. Who knows?"

He felt very sorry for Setona as he left her residence. She must be anxious over the possibility of war between the Ainus, her mother's people, and the settlers, her father's people. She and Tonkuru loved each other, Matsuzo was sure. If war broke out, there would be no hope of the lovers being united.

It was curious that she had also mentioned Okikumuri. Zenta had brought up the Ainu god during their last audience with the commander. It was a pity the Japanese in the settlement didn't believe in Okikumuri. They might think twice about starting a war with the Ainus.

TEN

Zenta was normally an early riser, but when he awoke in the morning, he discovered that Tonkuru and the headman had already left the house. Confident of his alertness, it shook him a little to learn that the two men could have got up and moved around in the one-room house without waking him. He must have been more tired than he had realized. Still, knowing that the Ainus could move so softly was a disquieting thought.

Mopi and her mother served breakfast to him, and the girl told him that her father and brother had gone to see whether the hunters had had success in finding the rogue bear.

As she watched him eat, she shyly suggested exchanging language lessons. "If your friend come back, I surprise him with new Japanese words."

Looking at her wistful face, Zenta could not tell her that there was little chance of Matsuzo returning to the Ainu village. "Thank you," he said gently. "I should like to exchange lessons with you and learn as much as I can."

The headman and Tonkuru returned just as Zenta was trying to finish his gruel of boiled roots. Not as sweet as yam gruel, it was filling enough, but had a disconcerting flavor of earthworms—not that Zenta had ever actually eaten earthworms, but he imagined the taste because of the sinuous shape of the roots.

Tonkuru grinned when he saw Zenta's face. "Don't finish the gruel if you don't want to. I'm sure my mother can find something else for you."

"Please don't bother her," said Zenta. He closed his eyes and swallowed the rest of the gruel quickly. It didn't taste so bad if he couldn't see what he was eating. "The gruel must be really nourishing, since you people thrive on it."

"We certainly do," agreed Tonkuru, who accepted another bowl of the gruel from his mother.

"Have the hunters found any traces of the bear?" asked Zenta.

Tonkuru looked at Zenta, and there was no

longer any humor on his face. "No, none at all. Some of them are saying that there is no bear at large, and that you've made up the story."

Zenta tried to control his frustration. "So you don't believe that the Japanese settlers have been attacked by a bear, or that there is any danger of war breaking out?"

The headman interrupted with a comment. "My father believes your story," Tonkuru translated. "He also believes that there is a real danger of war, and he is doing everything he can to prepare us."

But as Zenta had expected, he was not allowed to see exactly what the preparations were. After breakfast Tonkuru went to join Ashiri and the other young men. Left to himself, Zenta looked around for Mopi and found her busy helping her mother with household tasks.

"When I am older, I go with my mother to gather the bark of trees," the girl told him as she sat twisting strips of bark to make cords.

"Perhaps you can show me which trees have useful bark," suggested Zenta.

"Oh, no!" she said, shocked. "Gathering bark women's work. Men hunt and fish."

Chastened, Zenta left her to her tasks and went outside. After the darkness inside the house, the glare of the sun hurt his eyes. Squinting, he looked around and saw that no one was in the clearing, although he could hear voices not too far away. He decided to go exploring.

Following a familiar path, he soon approached the clearing in front of Ashiri's house. There was no point in going to the house, since he already knew that the Ainu was out, preparing for defenses against a possible attack.

Zenta was just about to turn aside when he caught sight of Okera coming out of the entrance with a basket over her arm. Again, there was something furtive about the way she moved. He remembered the night when he and Matsuzo had seen her steal into the house. They had come to the conclusion that she had been meeting a lover.

Was the woman going to meet her lover now? In broad daylight? It was risky, but with her husband busy, she might have decided to take a chance. Who could the woman's lover be, then? If it *was* a lover she was going to meet.

Normally, Zenta was not a person who enjoyed spying on a tryst between lovers, but he decided there was something here worth investigating. He gave Okera a start of some twenty paces, and then he began to follow her.

Zenta was a skilled and silent tracker. But in this unfamiliar country, with its unseen hazards, he was at a disadvantage. Mindful of traps, he had to move slowly and carefully. He decided to watch where the woman placed her feet, and then to follow her steps. But that meant he had to keep her in sight without letting her see *him*.

In this he failed. At one moment, she seemed to turn her head, and he ducked quickly behind some trees. He waited until he was sure she had moved on, and then cautiously peered out again. She was nowhere in sight. He walked as quickly as he could, without making too much noise. She was still nowhere in sight. He started to run, but then thought better of it.

She must have noticed him. If she decided to escape him, she would certainly succeed, since this was her territory and she knew it much better than he did. It was a futile exercise, and he had only started it because he had nothing better to do. He would have spent his time better staying at the headman's house and learning more Ainu speech from Mopi, even if it meant accompanying her on "women's work."

Having decided to return, he went back a short distance and came to a place where the path branched. Which way had he come? His attention had been so concentrated on tracking Okera that he had failed to make a note of this intersection. He took the right branch, hoping he had not made a mistake. A little while later, when he came to another branching, he knew that he had indeed made a mistake. The landscape in front of him looked less and less familiar.

Back he went to the previous intersection—or was this the previous one? Perhaps he had gone past an intersection without noticing it. This time he took the left branch, but after going for a distance, he felt that the landscape looked even more unfamiliar.

His heart began to beat faster. Panic brought inattention and confusion of mind, he knew. Zenta stopped and made himself breathe slowly and regularly until the panic receded. Think calmly, now. And his calm conclusion was that he was totally lost.

The stream—that was what he should try to find. He could always proceed along the stream, since he had fished there with Ashiri and knew the way back. And to find the stream, the logical thing was to go downhill.

Only it wasn't always clear which direction was downhill when the ground was almost level and trees were in the way. Zenta didn't know how long he had been walking, but he did know that he was getting very hungry, which meant some hours had passed. The sun was almost directly overhead.

Several times he heard bird calls, and the sound of moving underbrush—perhaps a snow hare or a deer. Human voices, that's what his ears strained to hear. What his eager ears finally heard, however, was not the sound of human voices. It was the last thing he expected to hear, the last thing he wanted to hear: the growl of an angry bear.

There was no mistake. He had heard these growls before, during the Bear Festival and during his struggles with the animal at the gate of the Japanese settlement.

The growls rose to a yowl of fury, and of pain. Had one of the Ainu hunters found the rogue bear and engaged in a life-and-death struggle?

Zenta's first impulse was to call out and tell the man that he was coming to help. But he remembered that the man would not understand him, and might even be distracted by Zenta's cry just when he most needed his concentration. It was better to go first and see how he could best give help.

Going toward the source of the noise, Zenta found himself climbing uphill. That was not surprising, since the mountains probably contained many caves, where bears would likely be hibernating. Perhaps he would now find out why this particular bear was at large, instead of sleeping deep in his cave.

He came to the top of a rise and looked down into a glen. It was a small one, almost completely hidden, and he would never have found it if he had not been led there by the growls.

Zenta had expected to see a man struggling for his life with a ferocious bear. But what he saw was a cage, somewhat larger than the ones in front of many Ainu houses. It was made of stout logs, with its bottom standing on a platform raised several feet above the ground. Inside the cage was a bear—not a cub, like the ones he had seen before, but a full-grown brown bear.

Standing in front of the cage was a bearded man poking at the captive bear with a spear. Zenta realized after a while that the man was not trying to kill the bear, since his repeated jabs were not delivered with force. What he was doing was deliberately infuriating the animal.

Curious, Zenta began to climb down into the glen. Then he stopped dead. Why hadn't he noticed it before? The man with the spear was dressed as a Japanese.

Zenta noticed something else as a gust of wind blew toward him. Above the feral smell emanating from the tormented bear, he could smell something coming from its human tormentor. It was a strong smell of something familiar—something that reminded him of home—no, something more recent than that—a bath, that was it! It had to do with the bath he had taken on reaching the

Japanese settlement.

He finally realized exactly what the smell was: the fragrance of the oil he had used to dress his hair after his bath. Like all Japanese men, he tied his hair in a tight topknot, and to make it easier to manage, he rubbed some oil into his hair. All Japanese men used oil for dressing their hair. No Ainu man did.

It was this hair oil that made the Japanese smell different from the Ainus.

Matsuzo was resolved to keep his eyes open and find out which of the settlers was responsible for the bear. Zenta would be impressed by his discovery.

But how to begin his investigation? When he returned to the lodging house for his breakfast, he found the other men looking at him suspiciously. They answered his greeting coldly, and some even turned their backs on him. They evidently regarded Zenta's departure as treachery, and Matsuzo, by association, was distrusted.

Jimbei seemed to be the only person who did not treat him as an outcast. He came just as Matsuzo was finishing his breakfast, and there was an apologetic smile on his face.

Matsuzo guessed what Jimbei's message was. "You don't have to tell me: I've been assigned to the moat-digging crew."

"Well, yes," admitted Jimbei. "The steward really wants as many men as possible on the job. With war looming, it's become even more urgent than ever."

Sighing, Matsuzo got up and followed Jimbei. He was not surprised. After the affair with the bear, he and Zenta had become heroes to the people who had witnessed the struggle at the gate. But now, following Zenta's desertion, Matsuzo had been demoted to a ditchdigger again.

Jimbei stole a look at the young ronin. "Mind you, I don't agree with the steward. You'd be much more useful as one of the soldiers. The steward may be proud of his military experience, but he doesn't recognize a good fighting man when he sees one."

The compliment flattered Matsuzo and lifted his spirits. It was true that Jimbei had shown interest in him and Zenta from the very first. He had supplied the map that had helped them to escape, after all.

"How long have you known your friend?" Jimbei asked. His voice was casual, perhaps a little too casual.

"Zenta? A little more than a year. We were both traveling toward the capital, and I asked him if I could become his pupil."

"Do you know anything about his background?"

In the course of their travels, Matsuzo had learned some of Zenta's history, but he saw no reason to satisfy Jimbei's curiosity. "I know very little," he replied austerely.

Jimbei did not seem offended. He flashed his familiar dimples and rolled his eyes. "Never mind—we all have our secrets. I won't tell you, for instance, how I left my own province and ended up here in Ezo."

They passed through the gate and reached the stretch of ground that had been cleared of trees and brush. Just looking at the ditch seemed to form blisters on his palms. Matsuzo sighed.

"I'll leave you to your work, shall I?" Jimbei said in a bright voice. "Maybe we can have supper together after you finish your stint tonight." He turned left quickly. He's probably afraid that he will be drafted into the digging crew if he lingers, Matsuzo thought sourly.

The first part of the morning was not too unpleasant. Wearing a hat, Matsuzo was simply one of several anonymous men, and he no longer felt like an outcast. He had been afraid for a while that his leg would be a problem. It had been healing well the last two days, and he didn't want to do anything to cause a return of the infection. But the work hardly affected his leg at all.

Most of the strain was in his shoulders. Soon he began to feel a twinge at the base of his neck, and then a definite ache. He was young and muscular. But digging the ditch required a different set of muscles from the ones used in his martial exercises.

The men took a short break when the gate opened and a pot, steaming invitingly, was brought out to them. It contained a mildly fermented drink made from millet. Matsuzo had drunk something similar made from fermented rice, but the Ezo climate was not suited to rice growing, and he was resigned to a riceless existence. Nevertheless the hot drink, sweetened and spiced with ginger, was very heartening.

Relaxed by the drink, the men began to chat idly. Matsuzo pulled his hat lower over his face and set himself to listen. The talk was mostly about the harsh winter and the lack of women. Matsuzo's attention sharpened when one of the men mentioned the attacks of the bear. They blamed the Ainus, and they all seemed to think that war was unavoidable.

All too soon the break ended and the men picked up their shovels again. Matsuzo discovered that his muscles, instead of aching less after the break, had stiffened painfully. Bending his neck brought red-hot streaks down his shoulder and back.

His neighbor in the ditch looked around when he heard Matsuzo's grunt of pain. "Your first day at this?" he asked sympathetically. "Why don't you stretch a little before digging again? It certainly helped me."

It sounded like good advice, and Matsuzo nodded his thanks. He was too embarrassed to do the stretching in front of all the others, however. Finally he retired to the end of the trench farthest away from the gate. There, the moat had already been dug to the proper depth and its sides shaped. Nobody was in sight, and Matsuzo had privacy for doing his exercises.

His first stretch brought more red-hot streaks coursing down his back. He stretched more carefully, and soon he began to feel his muscles loosening. While he was doing one of the bending exercises, he heard voices above him. They sounded like the two men who had brought the hot, spicy drink.

Matsuzo was just about to straighten up when he heard one of the men say something about a bear. The man was keeping his voice low, and he sounded cautious. Matsuzo crouched down again, flattening himself against the side of the moat. They wouldn't be able to see him unless they stood at the edge of the ditch directly above him.

"At this rate, we'll run out of the hair oil," said

one man. "We should bring a little less next time. Bears have very sensitive noses, so we don't need much."

"There won't be a next time," said the other man. "We don't have to get the bear maddened again, since the steward has almost convinced the commander to start the war."

"So!" said the first voice. "When do you think we'll mobilize our fighting men?"

"Very soon, I think."

The voices were receding, and Matsuzo stood up cautiously. Peering over the edge of the ditch, he saw the two men, still carrying the iron pot for the drink, disappear through the gate.

"I've been looking everywhere for you!" said a voice behind him.

Matsuzo jumped and looked around. Standing above him, on the other side of the ditch, was his neighbor. "Are you feeling better? I was getting worried."

Matsuzo climbed out and followed the other man to where the unfinished portion of the trench was. "I've been stealing a little rest," he confessed. "Your suggestion was good, and now I feel much better."

Physically, he really did feel better. Perhaps his muscles had loosened and become accustomed to the work. Mentally, he was deeply troubled. He didn't understand what the two men had meant by the hair oil, but they were certainly involved in some way with the bear. Moreover, war now seemed imminent. He had to think of some way to reach Zenta and tell him the news.

Matsuzo went thoughtfully back to his section of the trench. Most of the crew had almost finished their assigned work, but Matsuzo, having taken time off, still had a portion yet to dig. His good-natured neighbor was staying to help. As Matsuzo stood up to glance at the sky, which was turning pink, he caught a movement from the corner of his eye.

Without pausing to think, he threw himself at his neighbor and knocked him to the ground. Behind him he heard a low rumble, and as he lay with his face jammed against his neighbor's shoulder, he felt something hard strike the back of his shoulder.

The rumbling stopped and Matsuzo got up, wincing, to look around. A big pile of rocks buried the ground where he and his companion had been standing. He picked up a rock with jagged edges, probably the one that had struck his shoulder. If it had struck his head, he would have been seriously injured, or at the very least knocked unconscious.

His neighbor made wheezing noises as he struggled up. He finally found his voice. "I guess I have to thank you for pushing me out of the way." He stared at the pile of rocks. "Where did that come from?"

Matsuzo glanced up at the rim of the trench. "There was a piece of burlap earlier, piled high with the rocks that we threw up from our digging today. It's not there anymore."

The other man climbed up out of the trench and looked around. "I see the piece of burlap, and it's lying away from the edge. How do you explain that?"

Matsuzo knew exactly how to explain it, and so did the other man. Someone—possibly two people—had pulled up the far edge of the burlap, sending the pile of rocks crashing down on the two men below.

Silently, Matsuzo and his companion walked back to the gate. The other man muttered a hurried farewell and scuttled away. He had been friendly and helpful, and his reward had been a near escape from serious injury. Small wonder he was anxious to get away from his dangerous new friend.

Somebody had made an attack on Matsuzo, either to disable him or to kill him. Why?

He had just overheard a conversation between the two men from the kitchen who had brought hot drinks to the ditch-digging crew. The men could have caught sight of their eavesdropper afterward and decided he was too dangerous to leave alive.

But what was so significant about the conversation? Matsuzo tried to recall. They had said something baffling about the bear, and about hair oil, and then they had talked about the war coming soon. There was nothing particularly secret about the war. Therefore it was the information about the bear and the hair oil that was dangerous.

He was almost certain now that someone in the settlement was responsible for bringing in the ravaging bear, and that person didn't want him to tell the commander. Well, the man was too late, thought Matsuzo with satisfaction. Both Jimbei and Setona now knew about this theory, and the young woman would be talking soon to the commander.

Matsuzo reached a decision: He would return to the Ainu village. He would try to be reconciled with Mopi. The image of her glee at the Bear Festival was fading, and what he remembered more was the hurt in her eyes when he had turned away from her.

Most important of all, he would see Zenta again. He would make up for his desertion, for he could tell Zenta about his discoveries.

ELEVEN

I can't be lost again, thought Zenta. He was covering familiar ground by now. But it was getting late, and in the gathering darkness everything looked different. If he didn't get back by evening, he would die, for it was too cold to survive the night outdoors. Already, his fingers and toes were hurting with a fierceness that promised a good case of chilblains.

Things were beginning to be clear now. He had never understood why the bear had not attacked Matsuzo when his young friend had met it alone the first time. Now he knew. It must have been because Matsuzo had not washed or combed his hair for weeks, and therefore it had contained no trace of the hair oil habitually worn by the Japanese. The bear, smelling him, did not detect in him the odor that signified the hateful enemy.

The path was finally looking familiar, and Zenta knew he was not far from the headman's house. Moreover, he could move faster, now that he was close to the house and his feet would not be springing hidden traps.

He saw the outlying buildings first. By now he could recognize most of the buildings: the storage house standing on stilts, the bear cage—now empty since the slaughter of its inmate during the festival—and the shed where animal skins were hung up to dry.

Reaching the drying shed, Zenta hesitated. He had important information to impart, but whom could he trust? The person he had seen tormenting the bear was wearing a kimono. Although the man's face had been too far away for Zenta to recognize, he had seen the heavy beard and mustache of an Ainu. It could have been Ashiri or one of his friends dressed as a Japanese. It could even have been the headman. The only man it could not be was Tonkuru, who still had a very light beard. He had to find a way to see the young Ainu alone.

To his immense relief, he saw the figure of Tonkuru emerge from the main house. He seemed to be going to the latrine hut. Zenta cleared his throat.

It was a very faint sound, but Tonkuru heard it at once. He walked over to the drying shed, and when he saw Zenta, he smiled. "What are you doing here? Tanning skins? You were gone so long that I was worried."

"I have something to tell you," said Zenta. Taking a deep breath, he began to tell how he had followed Okera and found the hidden glen, the caged bear, and the kimono-clad Ainu man who was jabbing at the animal.

Tonkuru's smile disappeared. "You'd better come in out of the cold. We'll have to call a council of the kotan again and tell them what you have seen."

Zenta was so tired that he wanted to sink down to the ground and close his eyes. He was also conscious of his filthy hands, burning with scratches and throbbing with chilblains. But he drew back from the house. "Wait. The rest of the kotan might not believe me. I'm an outsider, after all, and they might think I made up the story because I want to prevent the war."

"*I* believe your story, and I will support you," Tonkuru said grimly. Anger glowed in his deep-set eyes. The secret plotter in the glen was trying to undermine the authority of the future headman.

Zenta remembered the way Ashiri's friends had taunted Tonkuru about his infatuation with Setona. Although he didn't want to hurt the young Ainu's feelings, he said, "The others might not believe you, either. Everybody knows that you are opposed to the war as well."

Tonkuru flinched. "My father would support me. And my brother might."

"Don't forget that it was Okera I followed," Zenta reminded him. "Perhaps she was acting on Ashiri's orders."

Tonkuru sighed. "Ashiri is a valiant man, but easy to manipulate." He paused, then said, "It would help if you can find the hidden glen again. Then we'll *prove* the truth of your story."

Zenta began to think furiously. "Yes! And it would be even better if we could trap the guilty man into revealing himself—in front of witnesses. I think I've got an idea."

Matsuzo decided to set out early for the Ainu village. He was not the first one up, for he could hear activities in the lodging house. There were the sounds of weapons being cleaned, polished and readied for war.

For an instant he felt almost wistful. Since early

childhood he had been trained constantly and intensely in the arts of war. The sword, the bow, and the spear: Together they formed the main interests of his life. And now, since arriving in Ezo, the only implement he had handled was a spade. Zenta, at least, had had an opportunity to use his bow and a spear—a fishing spear. Matsuzo's hands were itching for a good sword fight.

But could he really raise his sword against the natives? He remembered the generous hospitality of the Ainus, the intelligence and goodwill of Tonkuru. He remembered Ashiri's quiet pride in his fishing. He remembered Mopi's mischief, her laughter, and her tender concentration as she bandaged his leg.

He had to prevent the war. He had to return to the Ainus and warn them.

The best way to leave the settlement was to do it openly. As he left the barracks, Matsuzo saw one of the other lodgers. "I'm working on the moat," he said, greeting the man cheerfully. "Are you coming to join me?"

"No, I'll be busy sharpening swords," replied the man, and quickly walked away.

Matsuzo smiled to himself. Mentioning the moat was a good way to avoid questions, since nobody wanted to be recruited for the digging. He used the ruse again with another man.

It failed at the gate. There was a man there appointed as guard, and when Matsuzo mentioned the moat, the man looked at him strangely. "Nobody is working on the moat now. Haven't you heard? We're about to march out and attack the enemy!"

Then he stared even more intently at Matsuzo. "Aren't you one of the ronin who spent some time with the savages?"

"Exactly," Matsuzo said easily, trying to cover his blunder. "I've been assigned to go outside the moat and do some scouting. I know the ground, and I can make sure there are no hidden traps for our men."

Before the guard could say anything, Matsuzo strolled through the gate, trying not to run. He half expected to be called back, but he heard no challenge behind his back.

Once past the moat and into the woods, he sighed with relief. But he could not relax now. He had to hurry; otherwise he might be overtaken by a Japanese army.

At least he and Zenta were on the same side now. He had made a mistake in choosing to stay with the settlers instead of trying to help the Ainus, who were innocent scapegoats, but his decision to stay had turned out fortunate, for it had enabled him to overhear the conversation about the bear and the hair oil. He had proof now that at least two of the Japanese settlers, not the Ainus, had been responsible for the bear.

Before he had gone very far into the woods, the cold began to penetrate his cotton clothing. His feet, in straw boots, soon ached with a pounding pain at every step. He couldn't put it off any longer. He had to put on his Ainu cloak and boots.

Zenta had insisted on keeping their Ainu articles of clothing, saying that if nothing else, they would be of interest in studying how to keep warm in this harsh climate. Matsuzo had considered putting some of the native clothing on under his kimono before leaving the lodging house. But he couldn't bring himself to wear the scratchy tunic woven of tree bark fibers next to his skin again. Furthermore, he would look far too bulky and people would point to him and laugh. That he wouldn't tolerate, for he was proud of his trim, athletic build. In the end he had simply rolled up the tunic, fur cloak, and boots, and had taken them along. If anyone asked about the bundle, he had planned to say it contained tools, but nobody had asked.

Now he unrolled the tunic and put it on over his kimono, and then fastened the fur cloak around his neck. He winced at the powerful, feral smell of the skins. Wearing the Ainu garment over his clothes made him look like a fat rice dumpling with legs, but at least there was no one to laugh at him.

Next he removed his wet cotton socks and straw boots, rubbed some circulation back into his frozen feet, and thrust them into the deerskin boots. Smelly they might be, but the boots were warm and waterproof.

Putting on the extra clothes took time, and time was what he did not have. The guard at the gate had given the impression that the Japanese force would be moving very soon. How soon? Matsuzo knew he had to hurry.

"I still think it's too dangerous," Tonkuru whispered to Zenta. "Once our man knows that you've seen his hidden glen, he'll try to kill you before we can get to the cage where the bear is kept."

"It's the only chance we have," Zenta whispered back. "I'll be very careful, and besides, you can protect my back."

Early in the morning they had told the headman about Zenta's discovery of the glen and the captive bear, although they did not mention the figure with the spear and the smell of the hair oil. The headman had promptly summoned the adult males of the kotan to mount an all-out search for the hidden glen. The headman's brother, the hunter, wanted only himself and his helpers on the search, but Ashiri and his friends demanded a part in the hunt. Finally the headman had given the order for all the men to join the search.

Arming themselves with their bows and spears, the men soon spread out, although they could still hear each other's movements from a distance. Zenta carried his own bow, the long Japanese bow that had been rescued by Ashiri from the ship-wreck.

At first Zenta was careful to keep close to Tonkuru. As long as he was with the other man, no one could attack him and hope to escape un-detected. As the morning advanced, however, he gradually pulled away from Tonkuru, for he saw that the ground was beginning to look familiar. He was treading the same path he had taken while following Okera.

There! There was the fork in the path where he had stood undecided yesterday. He had finally chosen the right branch. Some distance behind him he heard Tonkuru say something about tak-ing a shortcut into the hills, but Zenta was not paying attention, for he felt now that he could find the way to the secret glen again.

"Follow me!" he called out. "I think I've been here before!"

Tonkuru was out of sight. Zenta should have waited until he had the young Ainu with him. But he was too eager to press on while he still remembered the way.

Lightly and quickly he bounded on ahead, and with each step the way looked more familiar. He recognized the second fork in the path, and yes, he had taken the left branch yesterday. That pine tree looked familiar, and also that rock with a depression filled with snow. Unless he had made a mistake, he would soon find himself on the overlook above the glen.

He had not made a mistake. He saw a patch of shady ground he remembered, where the snow had not melted, and there he saw the footprints he himself had made, still visible in the snow. He passed the snowy patch and found himself once more looking down into the glen.

The cage was still there, and he could see the dark-brown shape of the animal huddled inside. It was motionless. Nobody was there to torment it with a spear. Zenta pitied the animal, which should by rights be getting its long winter sleep instead of being forced awake and goaded into an unnatural fury.

Carefully, Zenta began to grope his way down. He suspected there was an easier way into the valley, a shortcut, but it might take him a long time to find it. As he scrambled down, however, he soon regretted his precipitous descent. The last stretch became first a slither, then a long skid. He arrived at the valley floor faster than he wished and ended in an undignified heap.

Breathlessly, he picked himself up and quickly looked around. It was very quiet. He had succeeded in arriving before anyone else. Then he heard the snapping of a twig, and knew that he was not the first arrival after all.

A burly figure moved out from behind some trees, and this time Zenta was close enough to recognize the bearded face. It was Ashiri.

Zenta was saddened by the discovery. He realized that he had come to respect the headman's elder son. He might seem moody at times, but Zenta had suspected that Ashiri was actually shy, and was trying to hide his shyness under a surly exterior. Training a bear to attack human beings, even the alien Japanese, was a cruel act, and Zenta had not thought that this big, laconic Ainu was a cruel man.

Ashiri slowly approached the bear cage. His eyes were very wide, but then Ainu eyes always looked wide to a Japanese. He put out a hand toward the cage, and then quickly snatched it back when the bear moved slightly. He turned to Zenta and said something.

Could Ashiri be asking about the bear? wondered Zenta.

In that case . . .

Above his head came a muffled wail, a slithering sound, and the next moment Tonkuru crashed down into the valley. Zenta smiled on seeing that Tonkuru's arrival was just as undignified as his own.

After he had scrambled to his feet and dusted himself off, the young Ainu looked at Zenta reproachfully. "Why did you have to choose this steep way down? You could have followed all the others and walked over the easy way!"

All the others? Zenta looked behind him and saw that Ashiri had been joined by his two friends. Nor were they the only new arrivals. On the other side of the bear cage was the hunter, Ashiri's uncle, and with him were three of his assistants.

The hunter spoke to his nephew, who answered back, pointing first to Zenta, and then to the cage. One of the younger hunters said something, and one of Ashiri's friends responded. It wasn't clear who was doing the questioning and who the answering. Inside the cage the bear stirred sluggishly.

"What are they saying?" Zenta asked Tonkuru.

Suddenly everyone fell silent. Into the glen walked the headman. He gravely inspected the

193

bear, and then turned and said something to his youngest son.

"My father says the bear looks too torpid to attack anyone," Tonkuru told Zenta.

"Tell him we'll soon convince him otherwise," said Zenta, and Tonkuru translated. He raised his voice, so that no one in the glen could miss his words.

Then Tonkuru went up to the bear cage and, with a coolness that Zenta would never forget, pushed aside the wooden crossbar of the cage, releasing the bear. The animal hardly stirred. The young Ainu put his hand inside his cloak and pulled out a small blue-and-white china jar with a stopper. The Ainus did not produce pottery, and the jar clearly showed its Japanese origin. Tonkuru said something, of which Zenta understood only the word *oil*. Then the young Ainu abruptly pulled out the stopper and, swinging the jar by a cord tied around its neck, splashed the liquid contents of the jar at the circle of men around him.

A hoarse scream came from one of the men— from only one man. It was the hunter.

He dabbed frantically at the stains on his sleeve, and then he looked up at the bear. The animal was still lying quietly on its side.

He was not slow, the hunter. He immediately

sniffed at his sleeve and understood the trap. The liquid was not hair oil but plain water. Understanding came too late, however, and he had given himself away.

Tonkuru was speaking to the silent circle of witnesses, and Zenta knew that he was explaining the significance of the oil jar. The hunter stood straight and proud during his nephew's accusation. When Tonkuru finished, the hunter's eyes flashed, and he answered in a few curt words.

The headman then addressed the men, and a fiery discussion broke out. Unable to stand the suspense any longer, Zenta approached Tonkuru. "What is happening?" he demanded. "Does your uncle admit to training the bear?"

"Yes, he knows he can't deny it," Tonkuru answered. "What he's saying now is that he did it for the good of the kotan." The headman next picked up a stick and drew a long line in the ground. The hunter strode quickly to one side of the line, while Tonkuru moved to stand opposite him on the other side. The rest of the men looked at the two antagonists and then at each other. For a long time, no one moved.

Zenta wondered anxiously if they were going to fight a duel. Tonkuru was no match for his uncle. Then he saw that the two antagonists were not arming themselves.

195

Suddenly one of the men, an assistant of the hunter, walked over to Tonkuru's side of the line. A buzz of comments broke out from the others. The hunter stood proudly and said nothing, but his lips twisted bitterly.

Zenta finally understood. They were choosing sides.

No wonder the hunter looked so bitter. One of his own men was the first to desert him. The crucial question now seemed to be which side Ashiri would choose. Would he side with his uncle, a proven hunter, or with a younger brother designated to be his future headman?

Suddenly Ashiri smiled. It was the first time Zenta had seen this dour man look completely happy. With a toss of his head Ashiri walked over to Tonkuru's side of the line, and immediately his two friends followed him. After that, the two remaining men glumly went over to join the rest. Whether they agreed or not with the hunter's view on war, they must have been disturbed by his treacherous methods. One of the things Zenta had learned about the Ainus was that they despised falsehood. The headman's brother now stood alone.

Suddenly a slight figure darted out of the woods and ran up to Ashiri. It was Okera, carrying a basket on her arm. She seemed to be pleading with her husband. When he growled angrily at her, she began to weep.

Zenta recognized the basket on Okera's arm. She had carried it on the previous day, when he had been following her. He knew what she had in the basket, and he knew he had to act without delay. But he was already too late.

The hunter grabbed at the basket and snatched out a blue-and-white china jar. Laughing, he pulled the stopper out and swung the jar by the cord around its neck—just as Tonkuru had swung his jar. But this time the liquid that splashed out at the surrounding men had the unmistakable perfume of genuine hair oil.

Seeing the horrified faces around him, the hunter laughed harder. The ceramic jar still dangled from his fingers by its cord.

In the cage, the bear raised its head. A growl sounded deep in its throat, and it sat up. Its eyes were open now, and they burned with the torment it had endured for weeks, perhaps months. The bear lumbered to its feet, shaking the whole cage with its weight. With a roar, the animal flung itself out through the open door and turned toward the hunter.

The hunter still had the ceramic jar dangling from his hand, and his fingers seemed to be tangled in the cord. Before he could free his hand, the bear lunged for its archenemy.

Zenta raised his bow, but lowered it again. The bear and its victim were so tightly entwined that there was no way he could shoot effectively. Like the others, he could only watch in horror as the maddened animal sank its teeth into its victim's throat and tore savagely.

Without warning, the bear dropped the hunter, who fell on the ground and lay ominously still. Perhaps the animal had lost its ferocity once its victim had become lifeless. Slowly, the bear looked around and considered. Despite the blood dripping from its jaws, there was something stately in its stance.

Zenta now understood why the Ainus considered the bear a god, visiting them in this animal guise. Perhaps that was why the hunter's scheme was such an unforgivable crime.

How did one persuade the bear to reenter the cage? wondered Zenta. Only the hunter knew, and he would not be able to say anything, ever again.

Suddenly the bear opened its bloody jaws and growled again. No longer a god, it had become an animal again, looking for a fresh victim. It now turned toward the headman.

This time Zenta did not hesitate. Prepared by years of relentless martial training, he lifted his bow, the six-foot Japanese bow that had taken all his strength to string, lowered it, raised it again, and shot the bear between the eyes.

The bear stood upright for a moment and looked around with a curious dignity at the circle of silent men. Then, shaking its head as if puzzled, it staggered back and crashed to the ground.

A shrill scream broke the heavy silence in the glen. Above them, on the shoulder of the hill, stood the small figure of Mopi. She was waving and shouting.

Tonkuru lifted his head and looked at Zenta. "She says that one of the women gathering fern tips saw a mass of men approaching. The Japanese have mounted an attack!"

TWELVE

*Z*enta looked down at the dead body of the hunter. "So he has succeeded, after all. He has provoked the Japanese settlers into starting a war."

Would Matsuzo be part of the Japanese force? No, that was unthinkable. Matsuzo might not enjoy living with the Ainus, but Zenta could not believe that his friend would take arms against his former Ainu hosts—against Mopi. Was there some way to find him and tell him about the hunter's plot with the bear?

"Is it too late to stop the war?" asked Tonkuru. "Can't we explain to the Japanese that my uncle acted in secret, without the approval of the kotan?"

It would be impossible to find Matsuzo. "I'll try to get in touch with the Japanese vanguard," Zenta said finally. "Perhaps I can convince the commander. He's sympathetic to your people."

Tonkuru spoke to his father and his brother. They seemed to agree with Zenta's plan, but they looked somber. Ashiri, in particular, hung his head low. His wife, after all, had been involved in the plot, and he still had to determine the extent of her guilt.

When Zenta left the glen, the Ainus were gathering up the dead body of their best hunter, a man who had brought shame to his people with his deceit and treachery.

Matsuzo knew that he had to proceed carefully, but he also knew that time was running out. So the war faction in the settlement had got the upper hand after all. Why hadn't Setona and Jimbei been able to convince Commander Kato that the bear had been deliberately let into the settlement? What had gone wrong? Jimbei had an ingratiating way with him and was persuasive, but perhaps he was too unimportant a person for his opinion to count. But surely Setona's words would carry weight with her foster brother. Could something have happened to her?

He forded the river, which he remembered as

the place where he and Zenta had last seen Tonkuru. After that, the ground looked more and more familiar. He was getting hot, and he was very conscious of the ridiculous figure he made in his double layer of clothing. Wearing his arrow quiver on his back under the fur cloak made him look even fatter. Should he stop and take off his Ainu cloak?

Then he realized that he had reached the very place where he had met the bear earlier. A chill passed over him, and he no longer felt like removing his cloak. Wearing the native garments would make him smell like an Ainu to the bear. Besides, there was no time to stop and disrobe. He could almost feel the Japanese soldiers breathing down his neck.

Above his own panting, he heard a crackling noise ahead of him. The bear! He was meeting the bear again!

Then he saw that it was a man moving rapidly and lightly. The man came closer, and he recognized Zenta. Joy poured through him like a draft of hot sake.

Without thinking, without watching his feet, Matsuzo ran toward his friend. Zenta saw him, and broke into a huge grin. Then his face changed, and he shouted, "Look out!"

Matsuzo was quick, but not quick enough. He

threw himself to the side—a fraction of an instant too late.

There was a hiss and he felt a thud on his back.

To Zenta, everything seemed to pass slowly, taking ages. He saw Matsuzo's approaching figure. He saw the trip cord on the path. He yelled a warning. It took Matsuzo at least an hour to reach the cord and trip it with his foot. Slowly, ever so slowly, Matsuzo swerved but could not escape the arrow. It sank in so slowly that Zenta could almost see it burrowing its way into his back.

Matsuzo lay without moving on the ground. How long did it take for aconite to work? Was there time to pull out the arrow and suck out the poison? Perhaps if Zenta extracted the arrow very carefully, only a tiny amount of the poison would enter Matsuzo's body.

Zenta took a deep breath, and ran over to his friend. It took him ten years to arrive. "Do you . . ." His voice was husky, and he had to clear his throat. "Do you feel anything?"

With great care, Matsuzo moved his head and looked up. "No, I don't feel a thing."

Perhaps the shock was driving all feeling away. Perhaps the poison induced numbness. Zenta knelt down and put his hand gently on the arrow. The shaft, like all crossbow arrows, was a short one. It was buried approximately a third of its length. It had gone in at an acute angle, and there was hope that it had given Matsuzo only a scratch. But aconite was a very strong poison, and even a light scratch could be dangerous—but not fatal, he hoped with all his might, not fatal.

"I'm going to try to pull the arrow out," Zenta said, keeping his voice level. "Do you agree?"

Matsuzo shut his eyes for a moment, and then whispered, "Yes. At least you won't be doing harm."

Zenta gave the shaft a small, delicate jerk. It was still firmly embedded—so firmly embedded that it must have sunk deep. This was a very bad sign. He swallowed, and again jerked at the shaft, harder this time. "Do you feel anything?"

"No," said Matsuzo slowly. "I don't feel a thing—truly."

Zenta was drenched in cold perspiration. He seemed to be encased in armor made of ice chips. Suddenly, he pulled hard, and the shaft came up in his hands. He peered at the arrowhead. There was no blood on it. Not a drop.

Zenta stared at the arrow. He stared at his friend. "Get up. Let me look at your back."

Matsuzo rolled over clumsily, as if his limbs didn't quite work. Slowly he rose to his knees, then to his feet. "I feel fine," he said in wonder. "I feel fine!" he repeated.

Zenta pulled his friend's fur cloak off, and then the tunic woven of tree bark. Underneath, he found Matsuzo wearing a kimono. Tied across the back of the kimono was a quiver.

He finally understood: The Ainu arrow, slowed by two extra layers of clothing, had embedded itself in the quiver. Matsuzo had escaped without a scratch.

"I'm . . . I'm not hit?" asked Matsuzo. "The arrow didn't touch me?"

Zenta's insides seethed and bubbled with glee. He began to sputter, releasing some of his fizzing laughter. "The arrow c-couldn't p-p-penetrate all your layers of c-c-clothing!" he finally managed.

"Well, I was cold," grumbled Matsuzo, putting his tunic and cloak back on. "But since the Ainu cloth was scratchy, I . . ." His voice began to tremble, and he couldn't go on. A snort escaped from him, and in the next moment he was howling and doubled up with laughter.

The two men eventually quieted, and for some moments they simply looked at each other, with a gladness too strong for words.

Zenta broke the silence. "Why did you come back? You missed Ashiri's cheerful company?"

Matsuzo smiled, almost shyly. "He's a lot more cheerful than you are, sometimes."

"It must have been a hard decision for you,"

Zenta said gruffly. "I'm glad you're here."

While giving lessons in martial arts to the younger man, Zenta had seldom shown his approval beyond a nod or a smile. He was embarrassed to see that his open praise reduced Matsuzo nearly to tears. He pretended to inspect the Ainu arrowhead.

Finally Matsuzo blew his nose and cleared his throat. "The real reason I came back is because you were right after all. The Ainus weren't responsible for the bear: One of the settlers is the guilty one. I'm certain now."

Zenta's jaw dropped. "Impossible! It was an *Ainu* who was responsible for training the bear: the hunter, Tonkuru's uncle. We caught him at it and he's dead."

"I don't understand!" said Matsuzo, staring. "I distinctly overheard a conversation between two Japanese settlers, and they were talking about hair oil and about the bear."

I've been stupid, thought Zenta. One of the Japanese must have been involved with the plot as well. The hair oil Okera had brought to the hunter had to have come from the settlement.

He suddenly realized that time was passing. "We can't stand here talking."

Matsuzo nodded. "Yes, we have to hurry. A Japanese force is on the march. That's another reason I've come: to warn the Ainus."

"We've already heard about the Japanese force," said Zenta. "I hope to reach the vanguard before they clash with the Ainus."

As they hurried, he told Matsuzo about the scene in the secret glen with the captive bear. In exchange, Matsuzo told him about hiding in the moat and overhearing two men discussing the bear and the hair oil.

"So we know who the guilty Ainu is," said Matsuzo. "Who is the settler providing him with the hair oil?"

"It has to be someone who knows the way to the Ainu village," Zenta said thoughtfully. He stopped, and the two men looked at each other.

"Jimbei knows the way," Matsuzo said slowly. "He even drew us a map."

"It's easy to underestimate Jimbei," said Zenta. "He looks so good-natured and harmless."

"He certainly asked me a lot of questions about you," remarked Matsuzo. "He wanted to know about your background and what you'd been doing."

Zenta turned to look sharply at Matsuzo. "When was this?"

"After you left," replied Matsuzo.

Zenta thought about Jimbei, the man with the dimples and the ready laugh.

"It's horrible to think that a war could start through a deliberate misunderstanding," said Matsuzo. He stopped and looked around. "By the way, where are we going?"

"I told you," Zenta said impatiently. "I want to talk to the Japanese vanguard before they clash with the Ainus."

"Then we're not going the right way," said Matsuzo.

Zenta frowned. He knew the route perfectly well, since he had gone this way twice already. But as he peered at the sun, he discovered it was not where he expected to see it. What had happened? Perhaps after the fright over Matsuzo's tripping of the spring bow, they had turned themselves around without knowing it. Or had they?

He was lost. Again.

They finally found themselves on a rise, looking down into the river valley. Once they got down to the river, they wouldn't lose their way again, because they could simply follow it downstream. Zenta wiped his brow and for the first time understood Matsuzo's constant complaints about the itchiness of Ainu clothing. Hot and perspiring, he felt a frantic longing to reach under his tunic and scratch his back.

Behind him he heard Matsuzo's labored panting as he struggled up to the bluff in his extra layers of clothing. Just as Zenta turned to speak, he heard voices below—many voices. He hurried to the edge of the bluff and looked down at the river valley. His heart fell. For they had arrived too late, after all.

Drawn up on one side of the river was the Japanese force, and in the woods on Zenta's side of the river were the Ainus. The natives were badly outnumbered. Numbers didn't mean everything in this country, however. Whichever side won the battle, lives would be lost—lives of their friends, both Ainu and Japanese.

The men in the Japanese force wore a miscellaneous assortment of armor, for they were settlers, farmers hastily organized into fighters. They did not look like men who were prepared to rush across the river into battle with an unseen native enemy. It was already late afternoon, and the failing light would give an added advantage to the Ainus, who knew the country. Was there a chance that the Japanese might not attack until the next day?

"The Japanese men don't seem eager to fight," said Matsuzo's voice behind Zenta. "Maybe we won't have to do anything. The Ainus will lead them through the forest a few times, and eventually the invaders will be ready to go home."

Zenta shook his head. "Somebody went to a great deal of trouble to arrange this confrontation. He's not going to give up until he provokes a fight between the Ainus and the settlers."

From the forest an Ainu figure stepped out, and Zenta recognized Tonkuru. The young Ainu was taking a terrible risk coming out of cover, but he seemed determined to speak to the enemy first. He did not possess the stature of his elder brother, or the hunting skills of his dead uncle. Alone and exposed in front of the enemy, he stood with the confidence and coolness of a leader.

"Men of the settlement," he said, "tell me why you come armed and prepared for war."

There was a stir among the Japanese. The men at the banks of the stream parted, and a figure stepped forward. It was the first time Zenta had seen Commander Kato on his feet, and his legs were so short that he was not much taller standing than he had been when sitting. Nevertheless he did not present a ridiculous figure in his breast-plate and helmet. He no longer looked either lazy or tolerant, and his lips were grimly set.

"I had hoped to avoid war," the commander said harshly. "But when you sent a mad bear to wound our people and maul our children, we could no longer remain passive."

"We admit that one of our men sent the bear," Tonkuru said calmly.

For an instant, the Japanese settlers were silenced by his bold admission. Then an angry babble broke out, one voice being louder than the rest. It was that of the steward, frowning even more blackly than usual. Commander Kato nodded and began to raise his war fan, a flat piece of iron mounted on a short stick, which was used to signal the advance to the troops.

Tonkuru's voice cut through the babble. "But we have found the culprit! Both he and the bear are dead!"

Again Tonkuru had succeeded in silencing the enemy, and this time the silence lasted longer. Zenta saw a figure come up to the commander, someone no taller than he was, but much slimmer—perhaps a page boy with a pale, delicate complexion. But from the deep-set eyes, Zenta knew the identity of the figure: It was Setona, dressed as a boy. She was leaning toward the commander and speaking vehemently to him.

The commander nodded again, looking even grimmer than before. "You fear our strength," he said, addressing the Ainus. "That's why you admit your guilt. Once we withdraw, how do we know that you won't train other bears, even more ferocious, to attack us?"

Zenta saw the truth at last. Setona had not used her influence with the commander to keep the peace. On the contrary, *she* was the one who was urging him on to war. *She* was the one who had secretly conspired with the hunter to train the bear. *She* was the one who had supplied the hair oil. The two men Matsuzo had overheard talking must have been Setona's servants.

Again the commander raised his war fan. The low afternoon sun struck the iron fan and turned it to gold.

It was the fan that gave Zenta his idea. He took a deep breath, raised his voice, and called to the Japanese force across the river. "I am Okikumuri, the god of the Ainu people. You are violating my land if you cross the river. Go back. Go back before I lose patience and shoot you down one by one."

Shouting broke out among the invaders, sounds of jeering that could be heard all the way up to the bluff.

The voice of the steward responded, "You can't frighten us with your fairy tales. As for shooting us down, your Ainu bow can't even send an arrow across the river!"

"What are you going to do?" asked Matsuzo as Zenta began to string his bow.

Zenta didn't answer. He was glad that the sun was behind him, putting him in silhouette. As he reached for the arrow he wanted, he could feel the perspiration coming down his brow. He hastily wiped it out of his eyes, for this was one of the most important shots he would ever make in his life.

"You're not going to shoot the commander?" Matsuzo asked hoarsely.

"Of course not!" snapped Zenta. "That would be the worst thing I could do."

Usually alert to any hint of an intruder, he was concentrating all his attention on his aim, and did not notice the approach of a figure coming up the hill behind him.

For the third time the commander raised his fan; this time Zenta let fly his arrow. It flew with a strange whirring sound. He had used an arrow with a bulb-shaped head, which was cut with slits producing the sound during its flight. This eerie whirring was meant to demoralize the enemy.

The whirring stopped abruptly as the arrow hit the fan with a clang, which echoed in the valley. Commander Kato cried out sharply, and for a moment Zenta thought that the worst had happened: that he had wounded the commander after all.

But no. The commander merely shook his wrist a few times and nursed it against his chest. The men around him broke out into an excited chatter.

"It worked," Matsuzo said quietly. "Look, the Japanese are moving back."

"Let's go down," suggested Zenta. The two ronin turned and began to descend from the bluff. Zenta thought he saw a figure ahead of him disappear into the trees. But it was gone before he could see who it was.

When they reached the floor of the valley, they saw that the commander had turned his back on the Ainus and was giving orders. His men began to retreat from the river.

Suddenly one figure broke away from the rest. Setona ran forward, splashing right into the river until the water nearly reached her knees. She raised her voice, and this time she was addressing not the Japanese, but the Ainus, her mother's people.

Zenta did not understand her words, but he understood her intention. She was trying to incite the Ainus to attack the retreating Japanese.

Tonkuru spoke to her, pleading, begging. But Setona's eyes flashed angrily. Her voice turned vicious, and she began to jeer. Zenta recognized one word: the Ainu word for hunter.

An angry growl broke out among the Ainu men. Setona was probably accusing the men of the kotan of lacking the hunter's courage.

Suddenly the young woman staggered. An arrow protruded from her shoulder. The Ainu arrow had flown silently, unlike the bulb-headed one Zenta had shot. No one ever found out who had shot the arrow, but Zenta later suspected it came from one of the younger hunters, who must have blamed Setona for persuading their leader into joining the plot; they took it upon themselves to avenge his death.

Tonkuru ran into the river and picked up the young woman just as she began to slide into the water.

"Maybe the arrow didn't scratch her," said Matsuzo. "Maybe it glanced off a piece of clothing, the way it did with me."

"She's dying," said Zenta. "The poison works fast."

In Tonkuru's arms Setona struggled to speak. No one else, Japanese or Ainu, attempted to intrude on the privacy of the two. Within minutes the young woman began to gasp for breath, and with a sudden jerk she fell forward.

Another figure splashed into the river, from the Japanese side. Commander Kato approached Tonkuru, who stood dazed, with the dead woman still in his arms.

"I'm her foster brother," said the commander. "I should like to see to her burial."

Tonkuru finally looked up. "No. She told me she wanted to be buried with those she regarded as her own people."

THIRTEEN

"Why did she do it?" asked Matsuzo. It was the day after Setona's death, and she had been buried in Ainu ground, as she had wished. Her motive was still puzzling Matsuzo, and he finally questioned Tonkuru, whom he found sitting alone by the empty bear cage outside the headman's house.

"Isn't it obvious?" Tonkuru said dully. "She wanted war between our people and the settlers."

"But she, of all people, had the most reason to want peace!"

"Because she's half Japanese and half Ainu?" asked Tonkuru. "Her father might be Japanese, but she regarded herself as wholly Ainu."

Matsuzo still didn't understand. "In spite of the fact that she grew up in the settlement? I should think she would appreciate Japanese ways better than anyone in your kotan."

Tonkuru looked down at his hands. "I think it's *because* she grew up in the settlement that she resented the Japanese more than I do. She must have suffered a great deal of contempt and discrimination."

"The commander was good to her!" protested Matsuzo. "He considered her practically a sister."

"It's true that he was fond of her," admitted Tonkuru. "But not many people shared his feelings."

Almost everyone in the settlement had referred to the Ainus as savages, Matsuzo remembered. Setona, with her unmistakably round Ainu eyes, was probably called a savage behind her back—or even to her face. Perhaps she had reason to hate the Japanese after all. "But could she really help her mother's people by starting the war?" he asked. "You could have been massacred!"

"You are quite wrong," Tonkuru said coldly. "If war had broken out, we would unquestionably have won. Both Setona and I knew it."

Matsuzo was doubtful. "You think you would have won, in spite of the fact that the settlers had superior swords and spears? Some of the men even had muskets!"

Tonkuru's eyes flashed. "We would have won not only this battle, but the war as well. That was why Commander Kato decided to withdraw. His men might have been frightened off by your friend's shooting, but the commander gave the order to retreat because he had come to his senses at last. He knew that with night coming and his men unfamiliar with the terrain, his army would have been slaughtered."

"And yet you are still in favor of peace," murmured Matsuzo.

"We might win this war, and the one after that. But someday your people will overwhelm us. It is best for us if we begin now to live in peace together."

The admission could not have been easy for the young Ainu to make. "You are sure, then, that the Japanese will prevail ultimately?" asked Matsuzo.

"I became convinced when I learned about the great famine," Tonkuru said with bitter certainty. "That was the winter when our people would have starved if the settlers had not given us grain, the same winter when Setona's mother was given as wet nurse to the commander. I knew then that your methods of cultivating the land would ensure the survival of your people in greater numbers than our ways."

"So you want to convert your people from

hunting and gathering to agriculture?" said Matsuzo. He approved. The Ainus would become civilized. They would learn to take daily baths, eat with chopsticks, and stop sacrificing bears—and Mopi's pretty face might not have to be marred by a hideous tattoo.

"I don't *want* to convert our people," cried Tonkuru. "We may lose our culture, perhaps even our identity as a people. But if we don't, we will not survive. And if we don't survive, neither will our culture."

Matsuzo saw the sorrow in Tonkuru's face and tried to give comfort. "Your people will be grateful to you in future years for saving them from extinction."

"My people will hate me and curse me," Tonkuru said bleakly. "I stopped them from waging a war they were sure they could win." He swallowed, and when he spoke again, his voice was husky. "You asked me why Setona did it. Just before she died, she told me. She did it for my sake."

Zenta was fishing with Ashiri when he saw Jimbei lurking behind some trees. It was the same place he had been hiding before. This time he stepped forward openly and walked to the edge of the stream.

Ashiri glanced up at the approaching Japanese, grunted, and went back to staring at the water. He no longer regarded the newcomer as a threat.

Zenta waded back to the bank and climbed up. "You seem to know your way here," he told Jimbei. "Do you often come this way?"

Jimbei's dimples twinkled. "It wasn't a daily routine, but I did come several times. I've always been curious about the Ainus, you see. Do you think they would let me visit their village?"

"I don't see why they shouldn't," replied Zenta. "After all, *we* have been staying here for many days."

They heard Mopi's high voice calling. Ashiri raised his head and answered. Then he plunged his spear into the water and came up with a fine, flapping salmon. Nonchalantly depositing the fish on the bank, he climbed up and joined the other two men.

"Lunchtime," announced Mopi, coming up and making admiring noises at Ashiri's catch.

"We've been staying in Ashiri's house," Zenta said to Jimbei. "His wife, Okera, seems to want houseguests. Perhaps he can't scold her when we're around. Mopi helps Okera to cook."

Jimbei stared at the girl incredulously. "She can cook?"

Zenta grinned ruefully. "We don't know if she

can. Well-cooked Ainu food and badly-cooked Ainu food taste pretty much alike to us."

Mopi turned around when she heard them talking about her. Zenta introduced Jimbei, and by the time they walked to Ashiri's house, she was chattering happily to him.

Matsuzo was waiting for them, and Mopi went up to greet him. Her reunion with the young ronin had been strained at first.

"You are not angry with me now?" she had asked tremulously.

Matsuzo had assured her that he was not, and that he had not left the kotan because of anything she had done. After a while his friendship with the girl had gone back to its old footing.

Now, when he saw Mopi talking with so much animation to her new friend, Jimbei, Matsuzo looked put out. "She's a bit flighty, isn't she?" he whispered jealously to Zenta.

"Maybe she just likes dimples," said Zenta. "Anyway, if we manage to leave Ezo, she won't feel so unhappy if she has a new friend."

The two ronin had tried to find a boat to take them back to the mainland, but so far they had had no success. Tonkuru turned evasive when they brought up the subject. He might feel friendly toward the two ronin, he might be grateful, but the good of his people always came first.

He wants to use us as liaison with the Japanese settlers, Zenta thought, and that's why he won't let us go.

In any case, Zenta was not sure he could manage an Ainu boat. The Ainus crafted heavy dugouts hollowed from single logs, and he did not trust himself to paddle down the river in one, much less cross the sea.

While Ashiri went to his corner to fix the shaft of his spear, Mopi began to prepare the fish with instructions from Okera. Ashiri's wife was no longer the shrewish woman Zenta remembered. The other women of the kotan seemed to be ostracizing her. He had since learned that she had become acquainted with Setona during her visits to the settlement to trade deerskins. That was how she had been able to get the jars of hair oil. She was not guilty of betraying her husband, however.

Tonkuru had told Zenta about Okera's role. "The silly woman thought Ashiri wanted war, because he complained so much about the settlers. When my uncle, the hunter, told her about his plan to train the bear, she was eager to help him."

"And Ashiri had no inkling that she was involved?" Zenta had asked.

"My uncle warned her not to tell her husband, because Ashiri is too honest and straightforward to keep a secret."

"She must have had a shock when she saw Ashiri side with you, not with your uncle."

"Ashiri may be moody and grumpy, but he's absolutely loyal," Tonkuru had said with obvious affection.

Since the death of the hunter and the confrontation with the Japanese force, Okera had been unusually meek and obedient to her husband. On sitting down by the fire pit, however, Zenta caught a flash in her eyes. She still had plenty of spirit left.

Jimbei joined the two ronin by the edge of the hearth. "I heard you say that you want to return to the mainland."

Matsuzo sighed. "I don't know when we'll find a boat to take us. Don't you regularly get supplies and fresh immigrants from the mainland? Maybe we can get aboard the next boat on its way back."

"The next boat won't come for some months yet," said Jimbei.

Matsuzo sighed again. "We'll just have to wait, then."

After lunch, Mopi and Matsuzo resumed their exchange of language lessons. He was her favorite Japanese again, especially after he had praised her cooking extravagantly.

When Zenta went outside the house, he found

Jimbei following him. His eyes were curiously intent. "You must have stayed behind in the village when our army met the Ainus."

"Well, we didn't want to get involved in the fighting—on either side," said Zenta, and managed to avoid an outright lie.

"You missed something," said Jimbei, his dimples deepening. "Okikumuri, the god of the Ainus, shot down our commander's fan."

"Really," murmured Zenta. "It sounds as exciting as a fairy tale."

Jimbei laughed aloud. "Strange, isn't it, that their god should speak not in the Ainu language, but in Japanese?"

"Perhaps he felt it important to be understood."

"It was a good piece of shooting, anyway."

Zenta knew it was the best shooting he had ever done in his life. Then he looked at the other man in surprise. "How did you happen to see it so clearly?"

"I was right behind you on the bluff. Didn't you notice?"

So there had been someone standing on the bluff behind them after all. "Why didn't you say anything?" asked Zenta.

"I didn't see any reason to," replied Jimbei. "I caught sight of you up there and thought I'd better investigate, in case it was an ambush. Then when I overheard you talking, I knew your intention was good." He paused. "I was particularly struck by the way you lifted your bow. You raised it, then lowered it, and gradually moved it up again until it was just the right height."

Jimbei ended his phrases with a particular intonation. Zenta had not noticed it earlier in his speech, but just now it was too strong to miss. Perhaps Jimbei had deliberately exaggerated it.

Zenta felt a tightening of his chest, for he recognized this lilt: It was peculiar to his home province. "Who are you?" he asked Jimbei.

The other man shook his head. "You won't know my name, since I was just a low foot soldier. Anyway, I left when your father died. But I recognized you, because of your archery style. Your instructor taught it to all his students, and he took particular trouble with you."

The two men walked on silently. Zenta felt the same heaviness he always did at the mention of his past.

Finally Jimbei broke the silence. "I will do my best to find you a boat. There's one that the settlers use for fishing. It will hold only a couple of people, but I think it will get you home."

Zenta turned to look at Jimbei. "You can get into trouble. Won't the settlers miss the boat?"

"I owe it to your family," said Jimbei. "Besides, who is to know I took it?"

Jimbei kept his word. He returned to the Ainu village several times, and gradually became accepted even by Ashiri's friends. One morning he drew Zenta aside. "I have a boat. Can you be at the beach this afternoon?"

Just before sunset the two ronin arrived at the beach, the same one where they had landed less than a month ago. They had debated whether they should say farewell to the Ainus, but decided not to risk it. Tonkuru might try to stop them, and Mopi might break into tears.

When they reached the boat, however, they saw Ashiri. He was standing next to Jimbei, and the two were actually talking to each other, after a fashion.

Ashiri turned to Zenta and gravely held out his fishing spear. "For you," he said in passable Japanese.

Zenta was moved, for he knew how much the Ainu prized his spear. "Thank you," he said. Then he took off his bow and quiver and presented them to Ashiri. "For you."

They got into the boat and prepared to push off. "What if you have to shoot another sea gull?"

muttered Matsuzo.

"We'll try to spear a fish instead," Zenta replied.

On the shore, Jimbei waved. "Good-by!" he cried in the Ainu language.

"Good-by!" cried Ashiri, in Japanese.

AFTERWORD

The Ainus are a race of people who inhabited Japan before the ancestors of the modern Japanese arrived. Just where they came from is still a mystery. They are now found on the northern Japanese island of Hokkaido (formerly known as Ezo), but there are many Ainu place names on the main island of Honshu, showing that they must have lived there as well.

Racially, the Ainus are quite different from the Japanese. Some anthropologists believe that the Ainus belong to the Caucasian race, for they are distinguished by their deep-set eyes and their unusual hairiness.

Like Native Americans, the Ainus live by

hunting, fishing, and food gathering. Before the arrival of the Japanese, the Ainu had no knowledge of agriculture, pottery, metalwork, or written language.

Because of centuries of intermarriage with the Japanese, fewer than 17,000 pure-blooded Ainus remain today. Many have taken up agriculture and have given up their traditional livelihoods.

Today a visitor to the model Ainu villages on Hokkaido can see the Ainus perform some of their ancient dances and rituals.